W9-DJJ-707

WHAT WE MUST SEE:

YOUNG BLACK STORYTELLERS

Books by Orde Coombs

Eastern Religions in the Electric Age (Co-author)

We Speak as Liberators: Young Black Poets (Editor)

What We Must See: Young Black Storytellers (Editor)

WHAT

WE MUST SEE

Young Black Storytellers

An Anthology Edited with

an Introduction by ORDE COOMBS

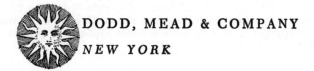 DODD, MEAD & COMPANY
NEW YORK

ISBN 0-396-06357-8
Library of Congress Catalog Card Number: 77-154062
Printed in the United States of America
by The Cornwall Press, Inc., Cornwall, N. Y.

Rites Fraternal by John Barber. Copyright © 1971 by John Barber. Reprinted by permission of the author. *Second Line/Cutting the Body Loose* by Val Ferdinand. Copyright © 1971 by Val Ferdinand. Reprinted by permission of the author. *Etta's Mind* by Liz Gant. Copyright © 1971 by Liz Gant. Reprinted by permission of the author. *Cheesy, Baby!* by R. Ernest Holmes. First appeared in *Liberator*. Copyright © 1971 by R. Ernest Holmes. Reprinted by permission of the author. *The Blue of Madness* by Arnold Kemp. Copyright © 1971 by Arnold Kemp. Reprinted by permission of the author. *Waiting for Her Train* by Audrey M. Lee. Copyright © 1971 by Audrey M. Lee. Reprinted by permission of the author. *The Pilgrims* by John McCluskey. Copyright © 1971 by John McCluskey. Reprinted by permission of the author. *A Word about Justice* by Thomas Muller-Thym. Copyright © 1971 by Thomas Muller-Thym. Reprinted by permission of the author. *The Fare to Crown Point* by Walter Myers. Copyright © 1971 by Walter Myers. Reprinted by permission of the author. *Miss Nora* by Lindsay Patterson. First appeared in *Essence*. Copyright © 1971 by Lindsay Patterson. Reprinted by permission of the author. *The Seed of a Slum's Eternity* by Eric Priestley. Copyright © 1971 by Eric Priestley. Reprinted by permission of the author. *A Right Proper Burial* by Alice I. Richardson. Copyright © 1971 by Alice I. Richardson. Reprinted by permission of Ann Elmo. *After Saturday Nite Comes Sunday* by sonia sanchez. Copyright © 1971 by sonia sanchez. Reprinted by permission of the author. *Harlem Transfer* by Evan K. Walker. Copyright © 1970 by *Negro Digest*. Reprinted by permission of *Black World*. *Sursum Corda [Lift Up Your Hearts]* by Edgar White. First appeared in *Liberator*. Copyright © 1971 by Edgar White. Reprinted by permission of the author. *Kiss the Girls for Me* by Wallace White. Copyright © 1971 by Wallace White. Reprinted by permission of the author.

Contents

Contents

Introduction

Why a new anthology of short stories by relatively unknown and unpublished black writers? Well, quite simply,
I happened upon this anthology, it was thrust upon me. I
was editing a book of poetry when a young brother sent me
a collection of his short stories. He wanted my opinion, he
said. He wanted to know if I thought he wrote well. He
wanted reassurance. In short, he wanted me to prophesy
about his future. Not only was I touched by his trust in me,
but I was overwhelmed by the quality and moral vision of his
work. And I was humbled. In the face of a blooming talent,
an editor, if he is worth his salt, feels a glow not unlike that
of a horticulturist when he stumbles upon black orchids in
a rain forest.

And so I had to do what I have now done. I had to collect
the works of young black men and women whose cudgels
were words, and who had to age quickly because the times

demanded it. Anthologies of short stories never seem to fulfill their promise. There is often too heavy a dose of eclecticism in the selections, or the quality of the writing passes gratuitously from good to bad, or the book tries to encompass too much and so engrosses no one. And this can happen even if one tries to run a connecting thread through the mosaic, even if one makes sure that the material is strong enough to bear sustained scrutiny. In the face of one's good intentions, one ends up with neither fish nor fowl, and quite often with pap. But I have tried, and perhaps succeeded, to give a sense of the feeling, the concerns, the insights of a generation of young people.

In none of these short stories is the specter of white oppression, or intrigue or rapaciousness more than merely menacing. The lives of blacks are still governed by white maliciousness. Less so, of course, but it is still a factor with which to contend. But these brothers and sisters have gone beyond pleas and execrations. They have gone beyond terror to find love. And this love is as clear as it is illuminating. It is the love for one's people; a celebration, as it were, of the infinite variety of a black life-style. And this is really what is important. This is what must be our beacon in the seventies. For if in our lives we have seen tragedy—and we have seen almost everything—if in our lives we have known bottomless despair, we have also seen us moving closer together as a people.

We now know that we are, in spite of the racists and the politicians, the false prophets and the hustlers, embarked on a voyage of self-discovery.

These short stories speak of the urban slums and the rural

farms. They speak of the abuse of a people who know hopelessness and fear and love. They speak of the harrowing search for identity, of growing strong, of being determined to live, and of fighting, ultimately, for one's life.

The stories of Lindsay Patterson *Miss Nora* and John Barber *Rites Fraternal* are set in the rural South, and though the cadences of the protagonists are different, their aspirations are similar to those who suffer in the hells of the North.

Evan Walker's *Harlem Transfer* chronicles the growing militancy of a father driven *sane* by a bureaucracy as numb as it is brutal. For it was the acceptance of his lot that was insanity, and only when he picks up his rifle does he see the pockmarks of his life, does he know finally, what he must do. And Eric Priestley, who is not yet twenty-seven, but who has seen too much blood not to have fought in a declared war, writes with the dreadful authority of one who *knows* what he has seen. *The Seed of a Slum's Eternity* is the story of a young man trying to hold onto his sanity, while all the symbols around him, beckon him to join the legions of the mad. Both Walker and Priestley know that the kinds of lives their people are compelled to lead add up to guerrilla warfare. And they echo the poet Carolyn Rodgers, who states in *U Name This One:* *

> let uh revolution come
> couldn't be no action like what
> i dun already seen.

---

* *We Speak As Liberators: Young Black Poets,* Orde Coombs, Dodd, Mead & Co., N.Y. 1970, p. 154.

And R. Ernest Holmes' story *Cheesy. Baby!* speaks of the fight to find one's own voice, to achieve an identity of one's own. Cheesy is half white, and he feels the rhythms, the joys, the pain of being black as keenly as his other brothers. But they will not recognize his quandary, they will not let him be who he wants to be. The poet Pearl Cleague Lomax, in *Feelings of a Very Light Negro as the Confrontation Approaches*,** describes the ambiguity, the terror of this no-man's-land:

> ... my pale skin and
> thin lips
> alienate me from my
> people.
> They are suspicious of
> my claim to
> blackness.
> They gaze into my pale
> blue eyes
> and they know that I have
> never danced
> naked and gleaming with sweat
> under a velvet African sky.
> But my soul screams
> against an alliance with
> you.
> I am Black inside myself
> and I hate you,
> for with your whiteness

** *Ibid.*, p. 12.

xii

and your power
you have destroyed me.

And R. Ernest Holmes makes us *feel* that special desperation.

And sonia sanchez in *After Saturday Nite Comes Sunday* writes of a sister who tries to shake the monkey off her lover's back. She fails, of course, but she will try again, and neither tears nor laughter have much meaning for her. Only the strength, only the determination to offer herself as the antidote to heroin; to sacrifice herself, if you will, for that black man in her life. As she stands, betrayed again, and naked to the Indianapolis winds, she is just part of that long, indomitable strain of our women who have refused to wallow in failure. For if one thing is certain, it is that we have endured; and if one thing is true, it is that we have fashioned from that endurance a kind of beauty that needs to be celebrated.

There is something very satisfying in trying to chronicle what is known as *The Black Experience*. For this is the time for energy, for the triumphant proclamation of the validity of a people's lives. Here, then, are sixteen black writers. They offer not merely hope or passion or despair or beauty. They offer us ourselves and they bid us be.

JOHN BARBER

Rites Fraternal

Li'l Willie Tee hastily grasped the doorknob, pulling on it angrily, to stop that bothersome rap-rapping, wondering "Who could this be, at this unholy hour, far past midnight, here deep in the dark heart of the wilderness?"

Jerking the door open, he found himself facing, tall and sharp-etched against the deep black Mississippi night, a white man. The man's pale, pink face was lit by laughing eyes and a big Cheshire cat grin. A "howdy" was followed by a fat, liquid flow of raw-edged, hard, northern-sounding words. "I am just a little old mailman. A twenty-year man for Uncle Sam's A-1, first class rural delivery service. Name's Johnny A. Freeman, from Minnesota, White Bear Lake, Minnesota. Ever heard of that place?"

"Naw, suh."

"That's way up North, of course. I'm just passing through. Can I stop in and catch a bite to eat and rest up a bit before

1

heading on down the road?" He brushed past the bug-eyed, wordless Willie, stepping into the two-room sharecropper shack, passing under the dim bulb hanging from the patch-broken ceiling and over to the room's side. Bending over he rolled his bulging knapsack off his back. Willie only then saw that he was carrying a red, white and blue sign attached to a broomstick-like handle. The man laid the sign down against the wall and Willie noticed the big blue letters emblazoned on it. Squinting, Willie puzzled out the letters, mumbling softly, "AH AM MAH BROTHA'S KEE-PA."

"Huh? Did you say something to me?"

"Naw, suh."

"Oh, yes. My banner. I am my brother's keeper. Yes, I am. I really do believe that. Try to practice what I preach, too," the words streaming forth. "Been doing it all my life, too. On this trip, I did it all the way from White Bear Lake to D.C. Struck out for Atlanta then to Vicksburg. It's kind of a reverse Sherman's March through the heart of Dixie. I'm trying to put out these still-raging fires in the hearts of men, black and white alike, telling my brothers everywhere that the war is over, let's get together and bind up the nation's divisive wounds, that sort of thing."

The fast-talking man paused, catching his breath, then started again, with a different thrust, one which Willie fully caught. "Well, come on. Let's get the fire going, the pot aboiling and let's you and me sit down and break bread together."

The short man followed him, obediently, toward the back, to the little room which served as combination kitchen and shed, the black host moving in a state of confusion tinged with fear. Two long strides into the kitchen's darkness, then the white man stopped short, silently bidding Willie to turn on the light. Willie stepped up near him, reached over him for the light's string which hung down on the man's face. Willie left him, white, blinking and standing there, picked up a bucket and headed out back to the well to get some water. Shortly after Willie had a good fire going in the old black, pot-bellied stove, a bucket of water bubbling and a pot of pork and beans heating up. Then the stranger sat at the kitchen table on a crate turned upside down, and bespectacled now, began to read his Bible under the poor light.

Out back, pumping water, Willie mused. "That sho is a funny man. He thinks he mah brother and mah keepa, and me havin' t' feed and bed him down, too. N'comin' t' mah door, past midnight, way down here in Liberty Bell County, n' on a dusty road way off the beaten track, too. Why, closes' town is Zion n' that's seventeen miles down the road, n' houses few and far between from there to here and from here to anywheres. N' he from that watertown place up North with the big white bear." Willie, laughing to himself and thinking, "White folks ways sho' is strange. Ah'll never understan' them, don' much understan' southern white folks, much less northern ones, n' Ah been tryin' to understan' these crackers down here all mah days."

Soon, they were . . . rather, the white man was eating, jaws churning a mile a minute. One, two, three cans of pork and beans emptied; two platefuls of greens and neckbones consumed; and a whole pie plate of corn bread. In addition, he

3

guzzled down cup after cup of steaming hot coffee, all the while talking, too. Willie had one cup of coffee before him, which grew cool, then cold, while he listened, comprehending little, watching that white man work his mouth wondrously, eating, drinking, talking. The black man wondered if the stranger's belly had a bottom and if anything could bridle his wagging tongue.

The white man rambled on: "Now, my favorite hero is John Brown, 'side from Johnny Appleseed and Jesus, of course." Suddenly he broke into a startling, but rich, melodious snatch or two from "John Brown's Body." Just as unexpectedly, he cut his song off, then ruminated some more out loud. He touched upon Jesus, then moved on to Thomas Jefferson and Abe Lincoln and George Washington and Iwo Jima and 1776 and San Juan Hill and voting rights and women's suffrage and back to the Blood of the Lamb. Willie kept eyeing him curiously, understanding none of the politics and history, barely more of the religious. He had never been much concerned religiously, anyway, and had blocked religion out of his mind entirely six years before, when those twin shafts of tragedy had struck him, taking Mae Sue, his wife, and June-boy, his son.

Finally, almost miraculously, the white man stopped, and, after gulping down the last bit of corn bread, yawned, saying: "Well, brother, let's go to bed. I'll sleep on the floor in the front room if it's all right with you, got my own bedding, underclothes, and wash-up stuff. Mean to make it to Mt. Zion before noon. Wake me up, bright and early, around six, will you? I got a twelve-thirty appointment with the syndicated press and TV people down at the county courthouse, concerning my Vicksburg voter registration and marching plans."

"Yessuh," Willie answered, vastly relieved for he, too, was tired and sleepy, and furthermore, he had only one cot, one sheet which wasn't too clean and one thin old army blanket. He had been about to offer all that to his guest, preparing to sleep on the floor, himself. The white man rose and proceeded to pull out a blanket and couple other things from his knapsack. Willie got into his nightclothes, slipped beneath the olive-colored old bed covering, waiting for the white man, thinking, "Ah wish he'd hurry up and pull that dadblamed string, shuttin' that light off so Ah kin get me some sleep."

Willie had to wait and wish a long while. His guest sat on the floor, Buddha-fashion, near the wall, put on his Ben Franklin glasses, read his Bible far into the . . . . next morning, and finally faded off around four-thirty. Even then Willie didn't go to sleep right away. He lay in bed, thinking hard, puzzling thoughts, not fitting any of the pieces together too well.

"In all these many years, Ah ain't never had no white night visitor. Kinda always feared havin' one, too, tho' this one here ain't what Ah was afraid of. Weird, tho'. He sho' is that. Wonder what he really doin' way down here. With all them funny i—deas. Any man, black or white, git himself killed talkin' like that in this here county. Well, that's his worry, ain't none o'mine. Let me git myself on out of this rut and catch me some shuteye. Gotta be up at five-thirty in the bright and early, feed the animals and plow me a lane or two. That weird man sho' got himself some fast-steppin' ahead of him, he gotta make seventeen miles in about five hours, and 'neath that swelterin' hot Mis'sippi risin' sun, too. Ha, Ah sho' don't envy him. Ah ain't done that long walk since Ah was a kid, nigh thirty years ago. That time Ah walked to Zion, and then hiked to Vicksburg.

"Ah gotta hitch up o' Beulah late tomorra mornin' n' git down to Zion maself, t' git me some mo' feed n' shells n' stuff down at Jenkins Dry Goods place. Wonder how Ah stan' on Jenkins' books now, reckon it's pretty bad, always is this time of year.

"White Bear Water Place. Sho' nuff mus' be cold way up there. Cain't stan' the col' maself. Onliest time Ah ever been out a Mis'sippi, come near freezin' to death. That cold winter in France, durin' the war. That awful col' night that time, in that French town on that moppin' up mission, me n' them freezin' black cats from Michigan n' California n' Jersey n' places, searchin' n' destroyin' them last minute stragglin' n' wounded n' desertin' Germans, takin' 'em prisoner n' everythin'. Mah hands all iced up, barely able to hold my rifle n' goin' down in that hole in the groun', n' that German youngun all shacked up n' sleepin' with that fat, pretty French gal.

"It was a touchin' scene, arm in arm, uptight together, keepin' out the cold with his big winter coat, servin' as their blanket, his pants off n' throwed to one side, his holster n' luger throwed to the other. Ah turned mah back on them, headed back upstairs, was gonna let somebody else capture him or shoot him or somethin' when all a sudden that gal

6

saw me, startin' screamin' like Ah was gonna rape her or somethin' n' me already aclimbin', me lookin' back n' seein' that German kid leap to the left for his gun rather than right for his pants, n' me with mah cold fingers n' all, lettin' fly with that clean n' true shot, strikin' temple, that white deer dead in mid-leap, so quick, so easy, a white man dead by the magic of mah frozen hands, mah fingers, mah eyes. That gal screamin' louder and louder like Ah was gonna sho'ly rape her now with her man cold dead n' unable to protect her now. Wasn't nobody could help her no way what with all them north'n black jittybugs upstairs killin' ev'ythin' white n' male n' uniformed they could see. 'Sides, one of 'em probably woulda give her some good warm lovin' like she never had befo', not even from them fairy Frenchmen. Not me, tho', Ah was raised right, n' in Mis'sippi, too. But, Lawd, Ah wish that German boy hadn' panicked. So young, too. Looked younger 'n me, n' Ah was only nineteen back in '44.

"Ah always could shoot good. 'Member that big white gen'ral pinned that pretty golden baby rifle on my chest in D.C. just 'fore Ah went overseas in '43. Ah was top shooter in the whole black segregated army, n' number three man in the whole army of millions of men, black, white, New York Port'Reekans, California Japs, Texas Mexicans, n' all.

"Maybe Mr. Freeman is that German boy—reincarnated, come back to get me." Willie jumped up, sweating profusely, feverishly, hot and scared, breaking for the far corner toward his rifle, stopped, saw and heard that the white man was soundly sleeping, snoring, in fact, oblivious to Willie

7

and the world. Relieved, Willie went back and fell deeply, coolly, asleep.

An hour later, Willie arose, dressed, went out, fed the horse, cow, mule and chickens, brought some more water in, washed up, and fixed a big breakfast for his guest, eggs, grits, pancakes, salted fatback, preserves, corn bread, milk and coffee. He woke his guest while he was cooking, heard him washing up, peeked in on him, reading his Bible, called him in to eat and sat down with him. The white man said grace and took up his fast-talking ways again, going right back to the same subjects. However, this time, when he was almost finished eating, the white man asked Willie if he was registered to vote. Willie's eyes grew. He blurted out, "Nah, suh, nah, suh, never will neither, suh. That's white folks bus'ness n' Ah knows mah place, right good, too, suh."

The white man, seeing Willie's face, eased around, fluttering, approaching his point from all sides, talking soothingly, coaxingly, compellingly, about democracy, sacrifice, one man —one vote, the precious blood shed to make Willie and the Negro people free. Freeman had shifted gears, becoming a smooth-talking evangelist, an openhearted, openarmed Jesus, pleading at the portals. And he beamed a broad smile an hour or so later, asking Willie to "go down and register to vote with me. Why, I'll walk all the way by your side and even call the Governor of Minnesota and even make contact with Washington to see that you are protected today and secured in days to come."

Shamefacedly, Willie said, "Ah right, suh, Ah'll go, but later this evenin' when Ah get down to Zion. Ah'm bound for

8

there late this mornin' anyhow. You go on 'head. Ah'll follow yuh. Ah'm comin' on with mah hoss n' buggy."

The white man smiled, taking Willie at his word, not knowing Willie would hardly refuse him, or any white man. Willie knew full well that the words that came out of his mouth had little to do with what was in his heart. He didn't intend to register or ever mess in that "sho' nuff" white folks business of politics. He knew better than that.

Then the white man, kneeling in prayer with his host, and praying out loud: "May the Lord watch between me and thee, while we are absent, one from another and bless you, real good," left. He had reached into his knapsack, extracted and gave to Willie three, shining, red apples and disappeared down the road toward Mt. Zion, striding long and fast, headed into the rising sun.

Three hours later, around ten o'clock, Willie hitched Big Beulah, his horse, to his wagon, and started toward Mt. Zion. About a mile away, just beyond the neighboring shack, Willie saw a crowd gathered in the middle of the road. He stepped Beulah even slower. He saw before him a crowd of about twenty people. His sharp eyes singled out Sheriff Simmons' white Stetson hat and Cap'n Jenkins' cream-colored cotton suit. There were also three big blue-coated, helmeted state troopers, a photographer, two men running around taking notes, and three young men across the road, playing catch with a basketball. Sheriff Simmons beckoned to Willie. He drew closer and saw what he feared, what he hated to see. There, lying in the roadside, face down upon the blood-stained poster, was the mailman from up North, who had eaten, slept, prayed with him and given him three apples. Blood ran down in a little rivulet from a temple hole, down his cheek, onto the placard, and onto the brown dirt.

Sheriff Simmons bellowed out to him, "Just keep goin' by, boy! This ain't yo' business. Hurry on to Zion or wherever you goin . . . an' git yo' goddam hat off in my presence."

"Yessuh," said Willie, snapping his hat off. However, instead of heading on to Mt. Zion, he turned horse and wagon around, not really disobeying, not even fully understanding what he was doing. He was sickening in his stomach. At first, he slow-stepped Big Beulah funereally, then, despite the heat, he hurried her home.

An hour later, drawn irresistibly to the spot, he was back. Everybody had left. The body and knapsack were gone, the picket sign and pool of blood being the only testaments to the tragedy. He walked slowly, ponderously, back a quarter mile and turned off the road, up the pathway to his neighbor's shack. He talked in low tones to the wide-eyed, frightened black man, the wife and children scared, hiding, peeking at him. He took a long, last look at their big black wall telephone, walked out on the porch, traced the wire from the shack to the pole on the road. His gaze followed the telegraph lines on down until they disappeared in the far North.

Willie went home again, going straight to his old footlock, searched for and found his old soldier's jacket, donned it for the first time in over two decades, a slight smile brightening his black face as he took note of the little golden medal, shaped like a rifle, and the many ribbons across his heart. He went out back, fed Big Beulah, the mule, the cow and the chickens, looked lingeringly across his fields of corn and cotton, half-owned by him with Captain Jenkins. He imagined Mae Sue standing in the doorway, June-boy playing in the bald-headed front yard. He smiled again, waved goodbye to all, started out down the road to Mt. Zion again, chomping on an apple, cradling his trusty rifle under his right arm.

Again he passed that awful spot. He stopped, picked up the bloodstained placard and walked on, in a hurry. It was near noon. He wanted to make Zion by four-thirty, thinking, "Gawd, it's awful hot, n' Ah gotta long, hard row to hoe, but Ah just gotta keep on keepin' on. Maybe Ah'll make it. Maybe Ah won't."

An hour later he saw the old 1950 maroon DeSota approach him. It slowed, stopped, a boy got out, the girl remained inside. The boy stood stockstill, facing him, his hands on his waist, glaring fire at him, trying to make him wilt or turn back. Willie kept advancing. The boy turned, ran back into the car, the exhaust pipes farted, the car wrenched around and raced off, shooting back gaseous malice. Willie smelled it, kept walking. He remembered. "That was one of the three boys who was laughin' and throwin' the basketball. Betcha he'll be back, fuh me." He went on.

An hour later, the same car came again. Three young fellows. The girl had been left behind. They stopped a hundred yards or so in front of Willie, got out of the car, each carrying a rifle.

Willie put down his placard. "They look like 30-30's," he said. "Good guns. Wonda' if them young uns can shoot good.

Well, whatcha know, that one movin' left is Cap'n Jenkins'
son. He served me all las' summa' down at the dry goods
store, nice kid too. Heard he was down at the univus'ty and
freshly married, too. Wish he hadn't come here. Always
treated me nice, tho'. Better 'n his daddy. Don't think he'd
even cheat me in the books like his ol' man. Ah was lookin'
fow'd to dealin' with him afta the ol' man dies. Kid movin'
right is one of the deputy sheriffs, mighty young to wear a
lawman's badge, but white folks know what they doin'.
Wonda why they splittin' up. Oh, Ah un'stan' now. They
gonna try to surroun' me. Well, first one make a rifle move,
Ah gotta shoot. Ah got the advantage, they's three to one,
that favors them. They's white; me, Ah'm a nigguh, that
favors them, Ah'm a nigguh with a gun; that psy-co-logi-kully
overrides all they advantages. They scared. Ah ain't no more,
n' never mo' will be neither. They completin' they triangle
now. If they make a whole circle roun' me, then they sho'
done got the advantage agin."

Young Jenkins forfeited the advantage. He panicked, lifted
his rifle too soon. He couldn't wait to get behind the nigger.
He didn't want to shoot the nigger in the back anyhow. He
figured it would have taken all the challenging fun out of
this Mississippi big-game hunt, black panther stalking, Africa
now come to Liberty Bell County. He lifted his 30-30 to sight
and saw no more, not ever again, the new gushing socket in
his head just above his nose, between his eyes, ending his
days of seeing, engulfing him in night, unending.

Willie had fired quickly, then whirled to his right, ducking
his head slightly, instinctively, hearing a whistling sound

brush past his left ear, and then firing again, without sighting, toward where the other shot had come. The young law-enforcer crumpled, heart hard hit just above his silvery badge. He fell back on his ass, sitting patiently, never to rise again. The third young man, the center one, who had brought the other two, suddenly dropped his rifle and fled to the car, showing his tail to Willie a second time. Willie smiled soberly. He took out another apple and walked on towards Mt. Zion.

He was surprised. He had expected the "young un" to come again, bringing back many more. He expected to be killed, going down with his rifle a'roarin' when they came. But nobody came. Now he was almost there. For the last two hours, a helicopter, dark olive-colored, had hovered above him, flying in concentric circles. He had kept his face upturned, his neck pivoting, his eyes orbiting. He expected it to swoop down, strafing. If it did, he was going to try to clip its wings, to fire away, and maybe make it crash into the ground in a fiery blaze. If it got him first, then he would simply be dead, which didn't bother him unduly. It didn't swoop. It merely kept circling him, while spiraling slowly back toward Mt. Zion. A gigantic, army-colored plane passed overhead. It reminded Willie of the big World War II bombers. "Maybe they's plannin' to drop a baby A-bomb on me or somethin'." He kept marching. The big plane flew on, unswervingly, seemingly impervious of him, sinking in the distance, down where the road pointed and Willie was headed. The helicopter kept circling above him, far away.

It was cool when he approached the town line. Down the

road he saw the waiting crowd. It looked to him like there
were about five hundred people. He petted his rifle, preparing to die, a soldier, striding on, shooting away. White-hatted
Sheriff Simmons and Cap'n Jenkins in his light suit stood out
in the crowd. He saw state troopers and soldiers. About ten
soldiers. "They might be sharpshooters like me," he thought.
"Well, if'n Ah can jus' git off two mo' shots 'fo' Ah die, Ah'll
be satisfied. Two easy shots, the targets promenadin' in white
like that. Cap'n Jenkins n' Sheriff Simmons standin' clear as
day."

He squinted into the distance, counting the soldiers, "One,
two, three, fo', . . . seven, eight, nine, ten exactly. Oh, well,
Ah'm a soldier, too. Ah'm ready, ready to go on home, to be
with Mae Sue n' June-boy, n' mah brother. . . ." Then he
heard it, rising from the crowd, big, booming, aimed at him,
shot straight, a loud, disembodied voice from some talking
machine down there in the heart of Mt. Zion, meant for his
hearing alone, his ears. He heard his name being blasted out:

WILLIAM! WILLIAM! WILLIAM TALIAFERRO, THE
FOURTH, LISTEN. THIS IS LEROY ANDERSON,
CHIEF UNITED STATES MARSHAL FOR THE WHOLE
STATE OF MISSISSIPPI. EVERYTHING IS GOING TO
BE ALL RIGHT IF YOU JUST LET IT BE. IF YOU
DON'T SHOOT ANYMORE, THAT IS. EVERYBODY
HERE IS GOING TO HELP YOU, OR IS BEING MADE
TO GO ALONG WITH OUR PROGRAM. I JUST BEEN
ON THE LINE WITH THE PRESIDENT AND THE AT-
TORNEY GENERAL. TEN SOLDIERS, INCLUDING

ONE COLORED BOY, ARE HERE, ORDERED BY THE PRESIDENT AND THE CHIEF OF STAFF, THE GREAT COMMANDING GENERAL, TO STAND BY YOU, GUARD YOU, MARCH WITH YOU AS FAR AS YOU WANT TO GO, ON INTO MT. ZION, ON TO VICKS-BURG, ANYWHERE. THE WHOLE COUNTRY, THE WHOLE WORLD IS WATCHING YOU. PICTURES OF YOU MARCHING HAVE BEEN FLASHED ACROSS THE WORLD BY SATELLITE TV. YOUR MARCH WILL BE COMPLETED. WHY, RIGHT HERE AT MY SIDE IS THE RIGHT REV. DR. MOSES ABRAHAM OVERCOM-ING, JR., THE GREAT CIVIL RIGHTS LEADER AND FRIEND OF PRESIDENTS. HE HAS A WORD, A WISE WORD TO SAY TO YOU. PLEASE LAY DOWN YOUR RIFLE.

Another voice rose, soft, southern, preachy, imploring:

YES SUH, BROTHER WILLIE TEE. EVERYTHING IS GOING TO BE ALL RIGHT. WE ARE REALLY ON THE WAY NOW. YES, SUH, BROTHER FREEMAN MADE THAT TIMELY CALL TO WASHINGTON, YES. THE SPIRIT OF BROTHER JOHN FREEMAN IS STILL MARCHING ON, WITH HIS SPIRIT ARE THE SOULS AND HEARTS OF FREE MEN EVERYWERE. THEY ARE COMING HERE FROM EVERYWHERE. I, MY-SELF, JUST FLEW IN FROM NEW YORK AN HOUR AGO ON THE PRESIDENT'S PERSONAL PLANE. I JUST GOT THROUGH TALKING TO HIM, TOO, ON THE HOT LINE. JUST TALKED WITH THE POPE,

TOO, AND THE PREMIER OF ISRAEL, AND THE
HEAD OF THE PAN AFRO-ARABIAN DELEGATION
TO THE UNITED NATIONS, AND THE CHINESE AND
RUSSIAN CHIEFS OF STATE. PRIESTS AND RABBIS
AND CLERGYMEN AND RELIGIOUS PEOPLE AND
EVEN UNBELIEVERS FROM ALL OVER THE WORLD
ARE JOINING IN, SUPPORTING YOU AND THE SPIRIT
OF BROTHER FREEMAN AND OUR MARCHING
PLANS. FROM FAR BEYOND THE MIGHTY AND
MAJESTIC WATERS MEN ARE PREPARING TO COME
TO MT. ZION AND MARCH ON TO VICKSBURG. IT
SHALL BE THE GREATEST NONVIOLENT MARCH
SINCE MOSES HEADED DOWN TO THE RED SEA.
MILLIONS WILL COME, BLACK AND WHITE, RED,
BROWN AND YELLOW, THE RICH AND THE POOR,
THE HIGH AND THE LOW, THE COMMUNIST AND
THE CAPITALIST, ALL COMING. GOD IS TRULY ON
OUR SIDE, SMILING DOWN ON US THROUGH THE
LOWLY, HOVERING WHITE DOVE OF PEACE. HE
HAS BEEN PROTECTING YOU BY HIS POWERFUL
SHIELD OF LOVE, KEEPING YOU ON YOUR COURA-
GEOUS JOURNEY, FROM ALL HURT, HARM AND
DANGER, WALKING RIGHT BY YOUR SIDE. I WANT
TO WALK BY YOUR SIDE, TOO. WE ALL DO. PLEASE
DON'T SHOOT NO MORE. YOU ARE A HERO, A LONG-
WAITED-FOR JOSHUA FOR OUR LONG-SUFFERING
PEOPLE, A GREAT SAMARITAN, SO PLEASE DON'T
SHOOT NO MORE, FOR YOUR SAKE, FOR OUR PEO-
PLE'S SAKE, FOR OUR FAIR AND LIBERTY-LOVING

LAND'S SAKE, FOR THE SAKE OF MANKIND AND THE WORLD. IF YOU SHOOT, OUR MAGNIFICENT CAUSE WILL BE LOST. MORE WILL DIE, NEEDLESSLY, IF YOU SHOOT AGAIN. BESIDES, THEN, SOMETHING NOT SO GOOD WILL HAVE TO HAPPEN TO YOU. OH, GREAT GOD FORBID. ON, MAY GREAT GOD CONTINUE TO BE YOUR COUNSELOR, YOUR UNSEEN AND SILENT PROTECTOR AND GUIDE. OH, IN HIS MATCHLESS NAME, LAY DOWN YOUR FIERY SWORD. COME ON, JOIN US AT THE MISSISSIPPI RIVER AND LET ME BAPTIZE YOU, AS THE ANGELIC HOSTS IN GLORY SING TRIUMPHANT SONGS AND MEN EVERYWHERE PAUSE TO BEHOLD THAT GREAT SCENE, WHERE MARCHING MEN AND WOMEN HAVE BEGUN EVEN IN THESE LAST AND EVIL DAYS TO STUDY WAR NO MORE. THIS WOULD BE THE WORLD'S FINEST MOMENT AND YOUR FINEST POSSIBLE ANSWER TO BROTHER FREEMAN'S PRAYERS FOR BROTHERHOOD AND PEACE. OH, WHAT A GREAT, NEW CHANCE FOR MANKIND. SO, BROTHER, PLEASE LAY DOWN YOUR RIFLE RIGHT WHERE YOU ARE. BRING ON YOUR BEAUTIFUL BLOODSTAINED BANNER AND LET US WALK TOGETHER.

Willie heard all the words, most of which made little sense to him, although he got the basic message. He did not even know who the Rev. Dr. Overcoming was and did not care, much less care about that white-man-voiced, Anderson, fellow. One thing was certain, he was not going to Vicksburg. That was too far away. He had already been there once years before, and had, absolutely, no desire to go there again. That marching stuff was somebody else's business. He had taken care of as much business other than his own as he intended to, toted the heavy burden about as far as he meant to bring it. He looked over to his right and saw the rusty sign above his head, nailed up a tree. He slowly pieced together its large white letters, fixing them into words.

"YOU . . . ARE . . . IN—TERIN' . . . MT. ZION . . . WEL—COME ! ! !"

"Ah gotta git on down to that voter registratin' office 'fo' it closes. It's in that big white buildin' jus' up ahead, looks like the buildin' on the back of a nick'l. Afta that, nothin' much matt'rs 'cept if Ah'm still livin', gittin' on back to mah hoss n' mule n' cow n' chickens n' gittin' 'em fed. This sho' nuff was a hard road Ah come down tho', jus' tryin' to keep faith with mah white brother. Well, guess Ah'm entitled to lay this heavy burden down now."

He dropped the banner, now rust-colored with dust and blood, its word illegible. He had brought it at long last within the legal confines of Mt. Zion. He raised his beloved rifle just a little bit higher, and head high, walked towards the town square. There the Mt. Zion road intersected the great Vicksburg Way. There also was the country courthouse. He meant to climb its marble steps.

He was still looking for any quick movements, swinging his sharp eyes right and left, noticing especially the left chests of the ten soldiers. These men stood in parade halt formation, each one wearing a gleamingly discernible emblem above the heart.

"If'n any of them sharpshooters jerks his shiny M-1 off the groun', Ah'm jus' gonna whirl n' shoot jus' below the rim of that pretty, tall white Stetson hat n' then, whirl n' . . . n' . . . n' . . . Suddenly, he smiled. And then, he grinned, as that mighty ocean of people in front of him, sharpshooters and all, began, magically, miraculously, to part.

VAL FERDINAND

Second Line/Cutting the Body Loose

Me, Ike and Pat with Betha just behind us walked down the street moving slowly with the band. The horn was high in the air and had a piece of purple, faded purple or maybe even blue ribbon tied to it. They were playing hard with their jaws puffed out and we walked beside them trying to catch who was playing what notes but we could not. The band moved slowly. We moved slowly and the saxophone began sounding like albert ayler, low and deep, full of shaky vibrato and feeling. It was a mournful sound. The player was old but the sound was surprisingly strong, especially coming out of a tarnished silver tenor that was held together with red rubber bands and played by the light brown fingers of a fifty-year-old negro man. He eyed me over his glasses, a white and black marching cap keeping the sun out of his eyes. We were turtle-marching our way out to wide orleans ave. and going pass the city's old audi-

torium and an empty lot where rev. somebody or the other
was in town holding revival services at night in what looked
like an old circus tent. The tent's sides were rolled up.

We could see jerome up ahead, his body dipping on the
beats as the old men played their dirge. I was watching
jerome march, his long body immersed in the flood of black
people dancing to some cemetery. Jerome had danced with
death prancing at his side innumerable times before during
the freedom rides and sit-ins when he was with CORE. His
raggity head, had been bloodied many times and his body
was used to trying jerking to relax beneath the crack of the
nightstick, jerking to bear the pain. Now he was bent at the
waist, mostly his chest was moving, and he was doing a step
that was probably as close to shuffling as he had ever come
in his life. Later after it was over, beads of sweat would
surface popping out from the dark of his black unshaded
head.

"Where you at?"

"Hey ma-an."

"How you feel?"

"Feel good. Good. Feel damn good."

And then our paths which had just crossed would have
uncrossed and i would wonder just how good he was really
feeling, would wonder if he had discontinued using the
medication he had to take to ease the mississippi pain that
still stung his body long long after every hamburger stand
was integrated or desegregated, as he would probably say.
You could tell it was jerome up their rocking back, lurching
forward and weaving in and out even though you couldn't

see his face, you could tell it was jerome just from the way his head looked (that is you could tell him if you knew him 'cause you would never forget the way his head looked, it looked like that; anyway jerome was up front marching). Jerome marched like how they march in church, dignified as they wanted to be and yet still at the same time, very, very down. The procession rounded corners slowly.

"They gon cut the body loose!"

One brother was running up and down the second liners explaining that they wasn't going to have to go all the way to the cemetery on account of they was going to cut the body loose. This meant that the hearse would keep on going and the band and the second liners and the rest of the procession was going to dance on back to some bar not too far away.

The marshal was out in front of the hearse, draped in a blue suit that was a little too big and too long but which was all the better to dance with. He wore yellow socks and brown shoes as a crazy combination of his own. After the body was cut loose, the steps he invented with his hat flipped jauntily over his forearm were amazing contortions of knees, shins and flying feet. He executed them with the straightest bored nonchalant don't give a goddamn look i have ever seen on anybody's face that was doing as much work as he was doing. He had somebody by him fanning and wiping his face after every series of grief-inspired movements. He looked so sad to be dancing so hard and making so many others of us smile as we watched him and tried to imitate some of his easier moves. He was the coolest person in that street marching toward a bar two blocks away under a two-thirty p.m. new orleans summer sun. The coolest.

We stood in line and the second liners were shouting, "open it up, open it up," meaning for the people in front to get out the way so that the hearse could pass with the body. After the hearse was gone we turned the corner and danced down to a bar where two of the younger black trumpeters engaged in a short duel at the bar house door. The older of the two won 'cause he not only had the chops to blow high and strong but he had the fingers and the knowledge that let you know he knew what he was doing when he began whipping out those crazy runs. You can't really describe it all, especially when we were marching and it seemed that all the horns were going for themselves but were really together. And free, wide open. Nowhere else were people dancing in the streets after someone had died. Nowhere else was the warm smell of cold beer on tap a fitting conclusion for the funeral of a friend. Nowhere else was death so pointedly belittled. One of us dying was only a small matter. Nothing could kill us all. Nothing could keep us contained. With this spirit and this music in us, black people would never die, never die.

An explosive sound erupted from the crowd. They began to answer the traditional call of the second line trumpet.

"Are you still alive!"

"YEAH!"

"Do we like to live!"

"YEAH!"

"Do you want to dance!"

"YEAH!"

"Well damn it, let's go!"

And the trumpeter broke into a famous chorus that was maybe a hundred years old.

"Ta-dant   Dant Dant
Dant DantdaNant
Ta-dant   Dant Dant
Dant DantdaNant"

An old bass drummer, his biceps knotted up beneath a sweat drenched white arrow dress shirt, was beating the cadence of his ancestors. A cadence, a sho' nuff for real live beat. A beat. A sound that set us jumping like beads of domestic sweat dropping on a greasy black hot skillet.

"BaBOOM BaBOOM
BabubuBOOM
BaBOOM BaBOOM
BabubuBOOM"

The trumpeter was taunting us now and the older people were jumping from their front porches as we passed them, and they were answering that blaring hot high taunt with unmistakable fires blazing in their sixty-year-old black eyes. They too danced as we passed them. They did the dances of their lives, the dances they used to celebrate how old they had become and what they had seen getting to their whatever number years, the dances they used to defy death. The hip shakings whose function was to lure men, demonstrate their loving abilities and make babies. A sixty-year-old

25

woman shook her hips and clapped her hands high over her head as our noisemaking passed her porch. She was up on her feet, a small child, perhaps her granddaughter was looking at her, and she was on her feet dancing, dancing for maybe a minute. Not too long but nevertheless dancing strong. We were ecstatic. We could see the bar. We knew it was ending, we knew we were almost there and defiantly we danced harder anyway. We hollered back even that much louder at the trumpeter as he squeezed out the last brassy blasts his lungs could throw forth. The end of the funeral was near, just as the end of life was near for some of us but it did not matter. When we get there, we'll get there. Meanwhile,

> "BaBOOM (tah) BOOMBOOM (tah)
> BOOMBOOM   BOOM
> BaBOOM (tah) BOOMBOOM (tah)
> BOOMBOOM   BOOM"

Black people look good. One of us dropped an umbrella and all went down real low like you do the duck walk but dancing and circling all around that umbrella. I looked at one brother who was on top of a broke car that was sitting on the side of the street, and he was doing something that might be what the original funky butt was like. Another brother in khaki pants was bent forward engrossed with shaking his butt up to the skies. Can jehovah understand this?

Where did we get all of this from, the marching and dancing and singing and togetherness. Africa can you hear us, do you know us, do you know our second line? Africa can you feel us, our palms clapping together, our feet slapping the asphalt and our throats pouring forth our vibrant cheers? Africa. Can you feel us? We can feel you. We jump with your spirits in us.

Our crowd didn't care what each other smelled like. We were all here for the same purpose. Whether it was wine or listerine on your breath didn't matter as long as you were breathing, as long as you were shouting out. And it didn't really matter if you used ban when you raised your arms to dance and wave umbrellas in the sun. And who cared what was on your feet as long as you kicked them high in the air and allowed yourself to rise and fall with the beat.

I looked at some of the white people who were there walking away after the band had gone inside, looked at them walking up the street away from all of that blackness, walking in the sun and looking so out of place looking at best out of place, looking like just what they are whatever that is. I looked at them going home to wait for another nigger to die and i wasn't even mad. I wasn't mad, not even about the cameras and tape recorders they had strapped to their bodies. It was just a lot better to be there to be in the procession instead of just there to watch it. Ike danced his ass off and Kush, who never usually missed a second line, got there late. Kush asked who had died and we told him we didn't know. We didn't know even though we had seen a small gold-framed picture being held out of the front window of the hearse by some relative as it passed by us. We didn't even know what instrument the brother had played.

The trumpeter was doing his crazy runs again and people were courteously pushing to get into the bar but they were letting the marshal, the relatives and the band go in first. The two trumpeters were the last of the band to go in. At the doorway they turned to blow their parting shots at us. And a duel began. People hollered out after the notes of which ever trumpeter they favored had gone ringing out, riding high over the telephone wires. I was laughing 'cause the older brother was winning. His last run had almost nearly followed the twisting quick kind of flight of a sparrow catching mosquito hawks at dawn except say the sparrow would have had to been as big as say an ostrich or something to match how big a sound the brother had. The loser ducked his head and went on into the bar. The peak of the older man's top lip was pink from the pressure of playing many years at different funerals and dances. He had been playing that trumpet a long, long time. I saw him smile as he had just bested the younger brother who looked like he was only twenty. Can you beat that, his eyes said? His black face broke out smiling. He had just played some horn. Everybody felt like laughing with him. We all felt good. The funeral ended with us smiling and laughing at each other in the street.

Etta's Mind

"I don't know why I even let you talk me into this, Etta! I'm 'bout tired as I can be! The baby was sick all day and I been cookin' and cleanin' and here I find myself followin' you out into the streets of New York in the pourin' rain to hear a bunch of ofay chicks talk 'bout women's rights!"

"Now you know Mrs. Sims will take good care of Willie Jr. Besides, look like you'd wanna know something 'bout your rights, Louise. Ain't you been kicked 'round enough by that no-count man of yours already? The way you always complainin' to me, seem like it's either this or a judo school!"

Etta paused in front of a small wooden newsstand and proceeded to dig a nickel and a dime out of the bottom of her brown Italian leather handbag. She hesitated, making a mental note to pick up the wallet that matched the purse. Suppose instead of getting wet on the corner of 125th and Broadway with Louise, she had been at some big downtown

luncheon with Eileen and the other Women's Lib Girls? It
just looked so country to be diggin' in the bottom of your
purse. . . .

"Well lady—you want the paper or not?"

The sound of their voices had awakened the grizzled little
old Slav who slept in the stand on night duty. Etta rolled
her eyes at him and threw the coins as hard as she could
into his dirty cigar box. She tucked the latest issue of the
Amsterdam News under her arm and hurried over to the
subway entrance where Louise was waiting.

The old fashioned wooden treadmill escalator bumped and
groaned as it strained its way to the upper level under the
weight of the two women. Etta carefully arranged her rain-
scarf over her freshly curled hair and complained: "Never
fails! Every time I go to that damn beautician, it rains! And
we would have to pick the only elevated part of the whole
New York subway system to catch the train! Hope they've
patched up some of the leaks in the roof up there!"

"Well, if you'da got an Afro like I been telling you to then
you wouldn't have that problem!" Louise smirked. "Besides,
all that pressin' and greasin' cost too much anyway!"

Etta sniffed in disdain at her friend's Afro and stepped off
the escalator. She threw thirty cents at the woman in the
token booth and swept over to the turnstile, her maxicoat
swirling behind her. Louise followed, also exchanging thirty
cents for a shiny token. She followed Etta through the turnstile and up the steps marked "Downtown."

They sat down on the edge of one of the dirty, scarred
benches.

"Did you see *Soul* on TV last night?" Louise shouted over the hurtling raindrops. "I 'specially liked some of them new Lee-Roy Jones poems! He did one with all this African music in the background—you know—that was outta site. It was all about . . ."

"Huh? What'd you say? Can't really hear you with the rain and all," Etta smiled apologetically. Louise nodded and turned a little so that she faced the lights of 125th Street.

What I wanna hear 'bout some ole *Soul* program when I got more important things to think about? I'm almost positive they gon' pick me to say a few words about Black female recruitment into the Movement at next week's big meeting and I only brought two people in the whole three months I been going! What'll I say if they ask me 'bout the Harlem participants?

She quickly pulled out a compact and peered at her face. Dabbing some powder on her nose she said: "You know Louise, a pair of these false eyelashes wouldn't hurt your cause none."

"And just what 'cause' you talkin' 'bout, huh?" Louise looked at her sharply.

"Well, you did say Willie's been comin' home a little late these past few days, didn't you?"

"But I don't see how no false eyelashes are gonna help that!" Louise answered with a short laugh. "What I need is some way to get that man a boss that won't drive him to drink. Ain't his time after five need changin', it's that nine to five horror he have to endure every day."

"That's just why I'm taking you to Women's Lib tonight!"

31

Etta burst out. "First it's excuses like that—the job's too tough, then it'll be somethin' else, then before you know it, he'll be dun spent the rent trying to chase his never endin' blues away and you'll be back to live-in-maid-three-times-a-week! . . . And I oughta know . . ." Etta laughed bitterly. "The same thing happened to that no good Bruce but I nipped that in the damn bud! I told him I didn't wanna hear that shit 'bout how bad they treated him on the job. He never listened to me when I tried to tell him 'bout those bastards at Macy's did he? I bet they beat me around just as much as his ole boss did! I told him if he couldn't be a man at home like he was during the day then he might as well just shack up with somebody else! There's too many weak niggers runnin' up and down the streets of Harlem as it is for me to be livin' with one!"

"But Etta, seem to me a man's gotta relax sometime. You can't expect him to be big and bad twenty-four hours a day can you?" Louise asked timidly.

"Well, I bet you Rockefeller or even Adamclaytonpowell didn't get where they're at by whinin' and cryin'! Shoot. They got out there and scuffled!"

"All the same, Etta . . ."

"All the same nothin'—a weak nigger is a weak nigger . . ." Suddenly Etta could see Bruce's eyes, warm and brown, slowly turning gunmetal black, and his hand, half raised and quivering as if awaiting the command to strike. . . . "Bitch, is love that much of a chore for you?" That was all. Then he had wheeled around and shoved his suitcase out of the gaping door and kicked it shut behind him.

She remembered how large tears had welled up and mixed with her mascara to form dirty gullies down her face. Three, four, five—yes, it'd been a good five hours before she even moved from the kitchen table where she'd been sitting. She had not gone to work the next day.

The noise of the train screeching to a halt jerked her back to reality. She raised the compact to her face once more. The hard, stiff lashes thrust themselves forward into the mirror for her examination. She blinked and they bowed at her command. Louise pulled her arm as the doors prepared to slam closed and she stepped on.

A blast of cold air made them both shiver as they made their way out of the subway onto the street. Louise grumbled, "What a night."

As they started to the renovated storefront that housed the downtown chapter of Women's Lib, Etta brightened perceptibly.

"You just wait 'til we git to the meetin'. Eileen and them others can explain everything much better than me! They say men want to keep the woman down 'cause they feels down themselves."

Louise looked quizically at Etta. "Don't nobody wanna be low man on the totem pole, Etta."

Etta rolled her eyes. "Now what's that supposed to mean?"

"Skip it."

The small 14th Street storefront that they finally turned into had once been someone's misinterpretation of a Village boutique. A few faded fashion posters still clung grimly to the dusty walls. The room was full of murmuring women and the sound of chairs scarring the wooden floor could be heard above their voices.

Louise headed toward a group of chairs near the door but Etta shook her head and proceeded to plunge through the crowd, waving and calling names as she went. The front row was filled so she and Louise took two chairs in the middle of the next row.

"That's Eileen, the chairman," Etta whispered loudly to Louise. "I'll introduce you to her later."

"Good evening, Sisters. My name is Pat Robinson, Second in Command of the Downtown Branch of the Women's Liberation Movement of New York City. You are all welcome. Now I'd like to introduce you to our Command Leader, Eileen Whitmore!"

Eileen bounded to the rostrum. "Good evening! Good evening! We have an awful lot to discuss tonight and little time to do it in so without further ado, I declare the meeting open. Can we hear the minutes of the last meeting?"

A thin redhead stepped forward and began reading in a high voice. When she was finished, Eileen bounded back to the rostrum once again. She read from a pile of newspaper clippings, introduced several people and then launched into a Welcome Speech for prospective members.

"Girls! Men are our enemies! They juggle statistics and tell us that women really control the economy, but why is it that we can't get executive positions in most of the firms downtown? If we can do the job why can't we get the same pay? Why. . . ."

Louise shifted in her seat and tried to concentrate. Drops of humid air fell on her forehead and she fought with her eyelids for control to keep them open. They drooped shut. She forced them back open. Shut. Open. She made one last vain attempt to keep them open, but their downward pull was irresistible. They shut. Then suddenly behind their shadowly veil she saw Eileen turn black. The hefty Command Leader seemed to fall to her knees in the doorway of a stench-filled cabin before the looming shadow of her white master.

"You my enemy, suh, and I knows it! But I'll go wid you if I has to. . . ."

Louise's head in sleep bobbed low, causing her to start. She blinked hard and remembering where she was, resumed her struggle for concentration.

"We are no longer mere chattel or sex symbols!" Eileen's booming voice continued. "We are tired of being portrayed on TV as glorified waitresses too!"

Little choruses of agreement blossomed and died around Louise. Intermingled with them she heard an enthusiastic "Right on!" from Etta.

The drops of heat fell faster now and Louise wearily began her battle once more. Shut. Open. Poor Willie. All alone. No—he did have the pork and beans I cooked and . . . Shut.

To Louise's bright dream world the enthusiastic applause that drifted through her subconscious was a shout of joy that rose up in the Quarters when the slaves heard the Yankees had won. "No mo auction block fo. . . ."

Etta gave Louise one last violent nudge. Louise's eyes flew open and her mouth which had been agape, snapped shut.

"We shall overcome!" They were shouting all around her. "Free at last!"

The meeting was over. Everyone stood and filed toward the door. Louise glanced fearfully at Etta but the latter had turned and was chatting gaily with the girl behind her. Once on the sidewalk, Etta turned back to Louise.

"The Girls want us to show 'em that new soulfood place on East 79th Street, Louise."

"Huh? Soulfood on the East side? But . . ."

"They'd rather not go all the way to Harlem. You know . . ." Etta gave her another nudge.

Louise looked over at their blank, smiling faces and thought —naw, I guess they don't.

They all piled into two of the Girls' cars.

Louise stood in the doorway of Soul East and stared. As the Italian headwaiter approached to show them to a table she whispered, "Thought you said this place was soul! Ain't nobody Black in here but you and me!"

"And the cook!" Etta whispered back as she followed the waiter to a large table. They were all seated, and as the waiter disappeared with their order Eileen, the Command Leader, asked Louise, "Why don't you tell us a little bit about yourself?"

"Well, there's not much to tell. I work sometimes as a

maid in Yonkers and my husband is Assistant Director of Mail Transport for the 72nd Street Branch of the Chase Manhattan. We live on 134th Street. That's all."

"That's very nice, Louise. We're so glad you could come because we need some advice on what to say at the meeting next week where all the Women's Lib chapters in New York will be coming together for our quarterly Progress Report on New Members." She tossed a string of brown hair out of her eyes and continued. "And we have to decide, among other things, on who is going to represent us on the dais. I'm open for suggestions."

Etta nervously fingered her imitation pearl ring, pulling the adjustable part of the band back and forth. After all the hands had been counted, "Well, Etta, it looks like you win."

Etta blushed and whispered thank you. She was so glad that Louise had been able to see her receive this honor.

"Now I'm sure you won't mind a couple of quick suggestions from us, will you? I didn't think so. Now Pat had a real good idea. She thought if you could get some statistics out of the Moynahan Report, you know, the part on how Black fathers are deserting their wives more than ever, that you could make a good case for Black women needing to be paid more so they can hire babysitters for their children when they go out to work. Sounds good, huh? And I was thinking that along with that you could add a personal touch by repeating that incident you told me about how your boyfriend told you he'd prefer you to stay at home instead of working overtime. And how he said you were always trying to boss him around saying you made as much money as he did . . . And how the bastard finally walked out on you in the middle of the night and. . . ."

"Uh huh." Etta nodded and glanced peevishly in Louise's direction. Louise avoided her eyes.

Etta forced herself to turn back to Eileen. She was still talking while four blonde and three brunette heads shook sadly in chorus. Wasn't that just like a man?

Eileen went on. "From all indications I would say that the Negro woman has just as bad a problem, if not worse, than her white counterpart. It's bad enough to be dominated in a chauvinistic male oriented society, but if you're also oppressed—well, I just don't know what I'd do!" The blonde and brunette heads shook in chorus again.

"Well—it ain't really all that bad!" Etta retorted quickly. "I don't think the Negro woman is any worse off than the white. We all got to fight these men together! But I thank you all for the suggestions. I'll do my best."

"Well, I guess that's all the business for tonight," Eileen said. "Let's order!"

The waiter cleared away the remnants of the ribs and feet they had tried to eat and the Girls prepared to leave. Louise still had not said a word. She put on her coat and followed Etta toward the door.

"You know—Eileen did come up with some good points 'bout Black men, what with her bein' white and all," Etta ventured as she opened the door.

38

Louise was about to respond when she looked down the stairs just in time to see Eileen run up to a tall young man with an Afro and a bouquet of flowers.

She turned back to Etta. Etta had nothing to say.

Cheesy, Baby!

It wouldn't have been too bad if he were light brown, but he was cheese-colored. Cheesy, that's what they called him, the ofay nigger. His given name was Anthony Narducci, the double c pronounced the true Italian way—the lips pushing out, then moving away from each other in the position of an open kiss to say "chi." One hell of a name for a colored cat, he thought.

His father was Italian, a painter, from Florence, and his mother was a large, black, bandanna-wearing woman from southern Georgia. It hadn't been too bad when the old man was around, but he had died, eleven years ago, when Cheesy was five. They had sort of made it when he was alive and stomping the turf because there was the Italian culture and all, and Cheesy was that "cute little tanned boy" of Mr. Narducci's. But when the old man faded from the scene, Cheesy became just another cream-colored son of a Negro woman, and it was the black life for them from then on: moving from downtown uptown, making the scene in the ghetto schools, the rats, the dope and the crumbling ceiling —the entire Harlem scene. And as if that weren't bad enough, no one even believed that Cheesy was the product of a sanctified marriage. They just took it for granted that he was an illegitimate child—the end product of a five-minute passion job in a cheap hotel between some no-count nigger woman and the first sloppy-assed ofay who had waved a five-dollar green in her face.

And so Cheesy came to hate his Roman nose and his thin lips. He didn't keep his thick, wavy black hair combed because he wasn't proud of it. He let it grow long and get messy. He was tired of being the brunt of the rank-outs, and the object of the finger pointing. He wanted to be black, black like the other guys. He wanted to bop with them and rumble with them, drink and turn on with them. But they always said, "Later, Cheesy, baby. You too pretty to corrupt, man. You don't want to run with us. So split the scene!"

But Cheesy didn't go down easy. To prove that he was a real soul brother at heart, he exaggerated everything that he thought he had to do to make the grade. He bopped a little harder, dipping the right shoulder low and pushing off on the ball of the left foot to get that rhythmic hop in his walk. He danced more seriously than the others, putting on minor performances each time he took to the floor. "Look out," the girls would say to each other, "Cheesy gonna smoke you off the floor!" He cursed a little more than the other brothers,

too. He had even chosen the blackest chick in the neighbor-
hood, Sarah Thompson, to be his girl.

It was the times with Sarah, when he was over her in bed,
that Cheesy forgot that he was thought of as white—when
his skin was in her skin, when he knew that he was loving
strong and that she was digging it because she was shipping
it back even stronger, when she was wanting it to end but
was trying to hold back because she was digging it so much.
And Cheesy always made love to Sarah bare-cocked, daring
life out of her, hoping to see the blinding result of what he
hoped to be. But never in these moments of passion was love
proclaimed for the girl enveloping him. Only on crowded
uptown streets, when blacks were everywhere, would Cheesy
feel moved to lean close to Sarah's ear and say: "Sarah, I love
you, baby." And Sarah never understood that.

All of Sarah's blackness hadn't done a thing for his position
with the brothers, though. He was still Cheesy to them. And
they put him down, saying that he was out of his natural
mind if he thought Sarah was his old lady because she was
in love with him; that Sarah was a phony chick, a proper
Miss Anne, who got her kicks out of sheeting with him and
running her black fingers through his fine hair; that he was
the closest thing to white that Sarah could find.

He stood now between Seventh and Eighth Avenues, leaning against the protruding tail fins of somebody's sparkling
white Cadillac, watching the Friday night whores prancing
and smiling, smiling and drifting into waiting barrooms.
Then he moved slowly up the block and stopped under the
marquee of the Apollo Theater to check the posters.

43

"Hard cats," he said, spotting a glossy picture of the Miracles. "Some wailin' studs!"

"Hey, Cheesy, baby! What you doin' over here?"

Cheesy turned to see Billy Washington's bearded face peering down at him. "What's happening, Billy? I came down to catch the show. Waitin' for Sarah now."

"Yeah!" Billy said, looking at a picture of the Supremes on the billboard. "Them babes is foxy as the shits!"

"Yeah, they some fine bitches," Cheesy agreed. He watched with admiration as the tall, bearded youngster moved under the marquee looking closely at the pictures.

Billy had a rep about having the best hands on 127th Street, and it was said that he was crazy enough to duke it with anyone, and good enough to come out on top. Just last week an ofay cop had surprised him and his fellas playing craps in the schoolyard. Billy had duked it with the cop and had knocked him cold. A right cross had done it. Bam! Just like that an the cop was decked out cold.

"You got some smokes?" Billy asked.

"Yeah," Cheesy said, reaching into his shirt pocket. "Here, man."

Billy pulled a cigarette from the pack and lit up.

"Take another one," Cheesy said. "You might get hung-up later on."

Billy smiled and pulled out two more. "Thanks, Cheesy, man. You awright." He glanced up the avenue. "So you still seein' Sarah, huh?"

"Yeah," Cheesy said, "we still makin' it."

"I swear, Cheesy, man. I don't know what you see in that

44

babe," Billy said, shaking his head. "I mean, a guy like you, you could pick up on any fine bitch you want—but you take Sarah, man. I don't understand it."

"It's working for us, man," Cheesy said, wanting to hurry past the subject. "What you guys got goin' tonight?"

"Working? *How's* it *working?*" Billy asked. "You keep pushin' peter and one day Sarah gonna plop a light-skinned reject in you lap!" Billy stopped. "And you wanna know something, baby? That's gonna make *her* very happy." Billy smiled and looked at Cheesy.

"What you guys got goin' tonight?" Cheesy asked again, almost at a whisper, his face an expressionless ashen reaction to Billy's truth.

Billy took a long drag, exhaled, and smiled. "Tonight, man, tonight we figure on busting some whiteys down in the Village. Yeah, man! We gonna kick some white ass tonight!"

"Yeah? Hey, Billy . . ." Cheesy looked up at his taller companion, his face working with excitement.

"Yeah, man?"

"You—"

"You lookin' *good*, baby!" Billy suddenly yelled to a young girl passing in a tight green mini that stuck to her thighs.

"You think I could rumble with you cats tonight?"

Billy's face twisted into a sour, disgusted expression. "Who? *You*, Cheesy? No, man, I told you about asking me that," he snapped.

"I know what you told me, but it ain't right, Billy. It ain't fair, man."

45

"Man, we gonna *fight* some white cats! We don't want one tailing along *with* us!"

"But I ain't white, Billy! My mother's as black as yours!"

"But you the same as white. If I didn't know you, I'd look at your mug and call you a pasty-face white bastard. You white, Cheesy. That's all is to it!"

"But I'm black in here," Cheesy said, pounding his fist over his heart. "I got as much soul as any black stud out here!"

"You got too much soul for your own good, Cheesy," Billy said. "Look, man, why you looking for trouble? You got a thing goin' for you in your skin. Go to college, marry some rich white babe, and live in Hollywood for the rest of your life."

"I ain't thinkin' about no college," Cheesy said, "and Sarah's good enough for me. C'mon, man, you cats been hard on me since I was a kid. Lighten up and let me rumble with you."

Billy took the cigarette from his mouth and dropped it lightly to the sidewalk. He watched the ash crumpling on the pavement, then destroyed the butt with his shoe. "O.K., Cheesy, man. Drop around in about two hours. We'll see what the fellas say."

Cheesy's heart was trying to break through his chest, but he maintained his composure, remembering that the game must always be played with a certain degree of cool. "Thanks," he called to Billy, who had started bopping slowly up the avenue. "Thanks, man. You'll see, you'll see. I won't let you down."

Waiting for Sarah to come, Cheesy couldn't stand still. He walked back and forth under the marquee, fingering the

46

blade in his pants pocket and feeling a new affinity with the passing black faces. It was a pleasant sensation, and so strong that when one of the faces smiled and nodded to him he almost rushed over and kissed it. After the face disappeared, Cheesy tried to remember whether it had belonged to a guy or a girl, and he was still looking after it when Sarah came and they went up to the balcony to dig the show.

While they were watching the cowboy flick, Cheesy told Sarah that he wasn't going to stay for the whole stage show. And she said, "Why, Anthony? What you got to do more important than to sit here with your girl?" Cheesy explained that he had to go somewhere, to meet the guys. And she said, "Guys? What guys you got to meet?" Patiently, he told her it was Billy Washington and the rest of the fellas, that they had something to do. She then wanted to know what they had to do, and Cheesy told her that it was none of her goddamned business, and that if she didn't stop Perry Masoning him to death he would go upside her head. And she told him to stop talking like a nigger to her. And he said, "I'm warning you, Sarah." And she said, "Awright! Go run with them reefer-smokin' punks and get yourself locked up!" And Big Baby B, the emcee, shouted, "Welcome all you swingers to the Big Baby B Show!" And Sarah said, "Why? Why you tryin' so hard to be colored, Anthony?" And he told her to sit still and dig the show because he didn't want to have to hit her, not right up there in the balcony. And some mar-seilled cats were doing splits on the stage, and Hully-Gully-ing. And Big Baby B said, "OHH-POP-A-DO, let me hear it one time for the fabulous Miracles!" And Cheesy got up to go, and Sarah grabbed his arm and said, "Please, Anthony, please don't run with those guys. You gonna end up just another finger-poppin', wine-guzzlin', nigger criminal!" And Cheesy slapped her hard across the mouth and ran down the stairs. And Big Baby B said, "I give you the Miracles!" And Sarah crying, called after him, "Anthony, Anthony, don't go baby, it's the Miracles. The Miracles." And Cheesy said, "Yeah, Sarah, give them three claps for me, baby."

They let Cheesy come because one of the cats said, "We can use him." The six of them split up into twos so that the Man wouldn't catch on to their program, and Cheesy went with Billy on the downtown IRT. Sitting across from them was an old white woman with a bag full of something, and she was looking over that something and smiling at Cheesy. And he was staring back at her and thinking, *Keep right on smilin', ofay mamma. You thinkin' I'm a handsome little white boy, huh? But you wrong, mama, cause I'm black, BLACK! This here's one of my soul brothers sittin' next to me, and we goin' bust some white cats!* He smiled back at her. *Maybe your son,* he thought, and suddenly laughed aloud.

Billy shoved him with his elbow, whispering. "Hey, man, what's the matter with you? You crazy?"

They met the other guys at Waverly Place in Greenwich Village. "We can walk free," Billy said. "They don't care down here." Then he told Cheesy what he had to do. "And talk white," Billy said, "talk white, man."

Cheesy wanted to object, but he let the matter drop.

The six boys lost themselves in the crowds for a few moments, then cut off into the West Village, along Hudson Street. Then Billy spotted three young men walking together and said, "O.K., Cheesy, there goes three white faggots. Do your stuff, man."

Cheesy broke from the others and walked up behind the three men. Then, in his best All-American accent, he said, "Gee whiz! So this is Greenwich Village. Where's all the fun they told me about?" The three young men turned to see who was talking, and Cheesy stared deep into the eyes of the blond one in the middle. "Do *you* know where the fun is?"

The young man looked down at Cheesy's thighs and said, "Yes, if you're looking for a gay time."

"I'm looking for a *good* time," Cheesy smiled.

"Then come with us."

Cheesy and the three young men walked into an apartment building on the same block, with Billy Washington and the rest of the fels watching. Billy cautioned the others to wait, and then he followed Cheesy and the fairies into the building, staying one landing behind so that they would not see him. As they were going into the corner apartment on the third floor, he saw the blond one drape his arm over Cheesy's shoulders. Cheesy turned around and smiled at the fairy, and Billy thought, *Man, Cheesy's playing the game like it SHOULD be played!* Then he went down to get the other guys, and they all went up to the third floor.

Billy knocked on the door, and after a while, one of the fairies said, "Who is it?"

"Telegram," Billy answered loudly.

Hearing that, one of the young men rushed to open the door, and Billy immediately stepped into the pad, put his knife blade against the frightened fairy's neck and said, "You fairy mother fucker, I'll kill you if you say one word!" The rest of the fels eased into the pad and followed the fairy who was trying to duck into the next room.

The blond young man had been leaning over Cheesy and getting ready to kiss him when Billy and the fels rushed in, and when Cheesy saw them coming he hauled off and punched the blond square in the mouth. The fairy fell back onto the couch holding his mouth and screaming, "You wop! You lousy wop!" Cheesy then smashed a left into the blond's gut and crossed with a right to the jaw, and the man's head shot back against the arm of the couch and his eyes closed.

Billy and the fels duked it with the other two in a corner until Billy knocked one of them out and the other pleaded with them to stop beating him. Billy tied the three of them together, taking the money from their pockets, while the other cats went through the apartment filling their pockets with whatever they could carry. Then they split down the stairs and walked casually to the bus stop.

A feeling that was close to love ran through Cheesy's heart when Billy said that they were going back up to his house to celebrate— to smoke reefers, guzzle some "Hombre," and maybe even jam a few broads. Cheesy was getting mentally high as they road back to Harlem, clowning in the back of the bus, sounding on the bus driver. He saw himself sitting with the fels, sucking on reefers, and tilting the bottle which had just come from another brother's mouth up to his mouth and letting the warm red liquid flush down his throat. They would be talking about how thay had made fools of the fairies, and Cheesy would be saying, "Hey, man! Didn't I play the role fine? And did you see me bust that blond in the mouth? Man, that's one fairy won't *ever* kiss anybody again!" He was already looking forward to the next episodes, when they'd go bopping not against any ass-switching fairies, but against a rough white gang in the Bronx, or maybe some P.R.s over in Spanish Harlem. Then he'd show the fels that they hadn't made a mistake in letting him run with them. And Cheesy was thinking, too, that it was time he put Sarah down and got himself a *real* soul sister. He figured that he didn't have to put up with her Miss Anne attitude just for the sake of her blackness any more. He'd get a chick that dug *his* scene now that the fellas had accepted him. Billy hadn't given him his share of the coins yet, but when he did, Cheesy would buy that stingy-brim hat that he'd wanted so much. He'd buy that and other things too.

"Slap me five," one of the fels said to Cheesy after he had sounded on the bus driver, and Cheesy started to bring his palm down upon the open palm of the other cat's. But just before they touched skin, the cat turned his hand over and said, "On the darker side!", and Cheesy slapped it on the top, and everyone burst out laughing. Cheesy laughed, too, and put his hands in his pockets.

They headed straight for the liquor store when they bounded out of the bus at 125th street, and Cheesy bopped as he had never bopped before. He yelled to the fine babes that swung past him on the avenue, and stared hate at the

Man who stood lazily twirling his billy stick like a drugged majorette on the corner. When people saw the six of them coming they stepped aside. *I'm in,* Cheesy thought, *one of the fels.*

Billy Washington went in to buy the wine because he looked the oldest. While he was inside, two of the fels picked up a couple of babes, assuring them, "We got much coin, much love, and gettin' something for the head right now!" Cheesy knew that before too long they would all be partying strong and that there would be some drawers copped before the night was over. He wondered which girl he'd get, and whether he'd be second or third in line. Billy came out of the store with three bottles in his hands and everybody headed for his house on 127th Street.

As they were walking, picking their way through the Harlem night crowd, Cheesy got to thinking about his knock-out punch and figured he'd ask Billy if he had seen him throw it. "Billy, man," he started, "did you see my knock-out punch?"

"Yeah," Billy said, "it was a thing of beauty. Where'd you learn to fight like that?"

"Same place you learned," Cheesy said.

"Yeah, man," Billy said. "Just like when Harlem was becoming a haven for niggers, blacks and whites was fightin' all the time."

"What?" Cheesy said.

"It don't matter," Billy said.

They walked in silence for awhile.

"Which girl am I gonna get?" Cheesy tried. His voice quivered as he spoke.

Billy shook his head back and forth in a slow but steady display of incomprehension. "Don't you see, man? Don't you *see*? Them girls ain't making no V-sign for *you*. Look around you. This is a time of symbols. "Here," Billy said, holding out a five-dollar bill to Cheesy. "We can use you again some time."

"Why, man," Cheesy said, ignoring the money. "Why it got to be this way?"

"Why there colors in the rainbow?" Billy asked. He dropped the five-dollar bill on the sidewalk and started away. A young, black boy who had been hovering near them, watching hesitantly, suddenly darted forward, scooped up the waiting bill, and disappeared.

Cheesy's steps slowed and the fellas began to pull away like an unremembered dream.

"Take it slow," one of the fels yelled back to him.

"Yeah," another brother yelled, "don't take no wooden nickels."

Cheesy stood white and rooted in the midst of swirling black folk, too dumbfounded to speak, looking at the bottles of wine tucked beneath his soul brother's arms, watching their trench coats disappearing up the avenue, and all the time hearing the blond fairy's frantic words ringing in his ears, "You wop! *You lousy* WOP!"

ARNOLD KEMP

The Blue of Madness

Blue is for death. Black the warm comfort of peace. Above, the sky hovered a pale shimmering blue.

Rich. Tranquil. Blue.

Manuel's eyes attached themselves to the hypnotic trace of color, and followed the vast plane from horizon to horizon; then, with a painful blink, clashed with the crude symmetry of earth and stone.

He shifted slightly on the cold ledge, the rough stone bit painfully into his buttocks. He shifted again, finding pleasure in the pain. I can feel pain, he thought incredulously, I can still feel pain. He leaned forward and the cold wind wrapped him. Down there were the heads, the mouths agape, the burning anxious eyes. Even from this height he could see the figures clearly. Each figure distinguishable in its hideousness. A pale blunt finger emerged from a tweedy arm and rushed up eight floors to prod his forehead. A thick tongue

55

flapped over drooping lips and the smack echoed in his brain. Heads bobbed at him; hands waved, beckoning, daring, negating. Mouths moved in heaving slurping gulps. He tried to shut it all out, away from himself.

His eyes netted a young pretty girl to the left of the crowd. Her eyes plunged at him in teen-age expectancy, the young breast heaving; her tiny hands caressing the tight yellow skirt she was wearing. The girl's mouth was a deep wound spurting at him.

"What do you want?" He screamed at her. "Go home! Go home you nasty little tramp with your yellow skirt and your ugly painted mouth. Go, and let me die here alone in the blue."

A sound to his left made him shift alertly. He threw his head up glueing his bony back to the wall, locking loose eyes to the sky.

"Hey, mister!" The voice called to Manuel tremulously. "Mister, here, the window to your left!"

Manuel closed his eyes. The black swarmed in quickly.

The blue. The blue would save him.

"Mister! here, to the left, my hand, mister, my hand!"

Manuel could hear the man's breathing, feel the tension twanging from the open window and along the narrow ledge. Manuel sat rigid. He had moved along the rough stone until he was safely away from all windows. There was only the corner of the building some twenty feet away, but there was no ledge at that point, so that was ruled out. He was a good eight feet from the window and its hanging policeman with hand and arm outstretched. The roof was eight floors above and below nothing for some glorious fraction of eternity. He would try to count them going down, conversely, like the space bugs: seven, . . . three, two . . .

"Mister! For Christ's sake, I can't hold this pose much longer. C'mon huh? Take my hand and let's go have a hot cuppa coffee and a little dinner, c'mon mister."

The policeman's voice wheezed in the cold. What was it —this intangible quantity that he couldn't order or shoot or club down, only grope for in awe? He was young and new on the force, his badge blazing, the oath fresh and burning in his breast.

He couldn't quite understand this situation. Waving to this damn crazy man and hanging from an eighth floor window with caterpillars dancing in your guts?

"C'mon mister."

The policeman's left arm, wrapped around a thin radiator pipe, ached. The ridged windowsill cut into his thigh, singing into the muscle, numbing his twisted flesh. The heavy pistol butt hooked into the wooden jamb at the turn of the window. He shifted. Earlier, his hat had blown off in the wind giving the crowd a thrill; a fired moment to oooOOO-hhh. It was then, that flashing moment as he hung groping for his hat with the crowd's breathless oooohhhhs rushing up and their tippling hearts waiting for him to soar down restringing the thin funicle of their own meager existence, that he, for the first time, felt sickly ashamed of the gun at his side, his oath, his very function.

The cop's arm ached, his thigh throbbed.

"Mister, please, lemme help yer, huh? Just talk to me,

okay? Give me yer name, yer reason for doing what yer doing. Anything. Just talk to me, huh."

"Say, Drake," another voice cut in from the hallway, out of sight of Manuel and the crowd, "mebbe he didn't understand ya. He looks like a guinea or a spick to me."

"That right mister? You Spanish? Hablo Espanol? Capeach Italiano?"

Manuel slowly turned his head and looked into the frightened young eyes. The policeman's face was puffy, the sandy hair jumping in the wind.

"You may tell your partner," Manuel said softly, "that I speak English very well thank you. I probably had a far better education than either of you." He turned his head back to the sky and smiled at his vanity. First pain now ego, he thought bemused. Watch yourself Manuel, another hour and you'll be contemplating tomorrow's breakfast or a Florida vacation.

A strong dirty wind swept in from the South bringing a stinging gritty soot with the faint smell of sulphur.

Down, down.

A voice called from the window; a heavier, nastier voice. Probaby his partner, thought Manuel, the one who said spick with such ease and familiarity. I should let him save me—what a joke that would be! Manuel chuckled, sucking grit between his teeth, through burning, cracked, peeling lips. No, he thought quite solemnly, it would be too good a joke to allow that one to become a savior. He would miss it, that one. There's no sensitivity in the voice, no hidden humor.

The joke would become a tragedy; irony is wasted on fools and brutes.

Manuel sighed, settling on the ledge as sand settles in an hourglass. The morning, cloudless and stark, slid across the sky with the ease of silk across the limbs of a lethargic lover. The sun was behind Manuel, hidden by the building. A dying, heatless sun, with only a sick white glare and thin, dust-filled streamers testifying to its sovereignty. On a higher ledge a pigeon fluttered its wings and white down rained, stirring the dust and soot. Manuel watched the feathers drift on and past him. It was that easy, thought Manuel. Just ruffle your feathers and shed it all. Ah, Ria, Ria, how easy it all is!

He began to think reluctantly of his wife, Ria; of the little ones: Juanita the beauty, the charmer with her mother's ebony beauty; of Carmen, the vixen, the little wild cat of Latin myth; and finally, his secret pride, little Manuel, the bright-eyed sensitive little boy afraid of everything, timid, shy, but so trusting, so curious and eager for love that he readily embraced everyone, his timidity submerged by the ready affection of his heart.

"My family," Manuel mumbled. A single tear slid from each eye, furrowing the brown skin.

The wind changed, lifting the sulphur and soot in a swirling sweep, leaving in its stead a sweet chocolatey redolence, an oily nauseous odor reminiscent of cocoa and castor oil. Manuel burped loudly. The pigeons stirred again and the muffled swish of warm bedclothes against bare skin encroached upon the ledge. Manuel squeezed his lids tightly against the tears.

"No," Manuel whimpered on the cold ledge, "No."

"Hey, buddy, ya just take it easy, huh? Don't worry, we sent for sumbody that can help ya, so just ya take it easy."

Manuel stared at the cop's ugly face, felt the pressure building up, gagging him. With a small cry he doubled forward, throwing up. The bile burst from his lips like charged magma, coated the chocolate-dipped wind and floated to the crowd: manna to the famished.

The movement was cataclysmic, throwing Manuel far forward, bringing screams from the crowd beneath. Manuel could feel the skin of his hands ripping on the rough sandstone. For a slight wavering second the equilibrium was broken; he pitched forward, the building surged; the crowd zoomed in and the wind roared through his head in a blasting pitch; then miraculously, and unwilled, he was back on the ledge, hollow eyes glued to the shimmering blue, his thin frame sweat-drenched in the cold air.

The girl's hair was a tousled bun of brown curls that kept falling in her eyes and blotting out the man sitting on the ledge. She pulled the sweater tight across her breast and smoothed the yellow skirt over her thighs. Icy air whistled up her little nose and popped warm out of parted orange lips. She stared, mesmerized, waiting, feeling an acute prickling at the base of her belly, a slight itch at the curved vee of her groin. She had never seen a man die. Never witnessed anything more brutal than a mild fist fight (which she had gleefully instigated); but she had read a lot and saw all the movies, TV shows, everything that had to do with death and violent assault. She would lie awake nights, her hazel eyes stretched, drawn to the clear screen of the ceiling, watching herself being beaten, stabbed, ravaged. And once, a week ago, she had been dragged to a dingy roof, raped, stomped and tossed off, her screams smearing the night blood-red. She had groveled on the drenched sheets as her tender, broken body had smacked into the asphalt with a dull splattering thud. She now groveled much the same way, the plump body fighting the smooth yellow skirt and sweater. There was a tightness in her chest. She wanted to tear off the sweater, the slip, brassiere, all that constrained and prevented the thrusting demon within from plunging forth, giving peace.

The heavy tweed topcoat weighed heavily on the man's shoulders and he shifted his weight often, trying to balance the discomfort. He looked quickly at his watch: one-thirty! My God! I told Kate noon. But she'll understand, Kate always does. I'll just tell her I was held up by business. Why the hell doesn't the fellow jump if he's going to? Wonder what his reasons are? A woman? Perhaps. But more than likely it's money. Once you have money the women come easy.

He shifted his weight again, juggling the coat's bulk and straightened the grey fedora on the balding, grey head. A soft pressure washed his side causing him to lower his eyes from the ledge.

She was in tight against him, the crowd pushing. Her

61

cute young face was pinched and drained; a wild gloss in her eyes. Her spreading fingers were running the breadth of belly and thigh, pressing, squeezing, digging. The yellow skirt was mottled and creased with dark grip-marks. She was a pretty thing, small and plump. Young. He took a quick look around the crowd, the fedora wobbling. All eyes were riveted to the ledge. Very gently the man eased his tweedy sheath behind the girl, sliding his palms down until they were even with the curved dips of the yellow skirt. Ever so slowly, he leaned forward until he was flush against the firm young flesh, could feel the resilience of her cheeks. Sweating, frightened, he waited breathlessly for the girl's angry turn, the rebuttal; the embarrassment and stammering apology he would make. To his surprise she pressed back almost in reciprocation! He shivered, hearing her heavy breathing synchronizing with his own laborious gulps. Again slowly, imperceptibly, he turned the palms of his hands outward until they cupped the round, spongy spheres from the bulging curve to the maddening cavity.

Off to the side someone hollered: "Jump ya bastard!" Immediately it was picked up, and people began clapping in time: jump, jump, jump. The girl shuddered. The man cursed. Together they began to sway with the crowd and the haunting chant.

The old woman, wearing a bulky green tweed coat full of dry-rot, buried her head in the bag sobbing. "Why doesn't somebody do something?" She cried. "That poor man. Why doesn't someone help him?"

The red headed man next to her laughed, twisted his thin

lips and spit around a chewed cigar. "Aw, take it easy, grandma. That bum ain't gone do nuttin', prob'ly tanked up on wine and wants a coupla meals and a little notoriety at the expense of the country."

"I don't think so," said a collegiate-looking young man wearing glasses and a bulky sweater with a big green "A" emblazoned on it. "It's a woman; his wife or his girl may have left him. It's always a woman."

"Like hell!" said a fat blonde woman. "Not in this town. Too many broads willing to help 'im forget. It's probably money."

The collegiate young man looked at her distastefully. "Really miss, why should a man kill himself over money—especially in this barbarous fashion. It seems quite obvious that if a man's only need is money it would be much simpler to merely go into a bank of some sort with a bomb or something and demand some. At least then there would be a reasonable chance for both gain and escape, and the most he could possibly lose is what he has already committed—his life."

"You're right sonny!" shot back the redheaded man. "It's probably a dame. The sumabitch wants to get his pitcher in the paper and cop a little sympathy."

"You're both nuts!" cried the fat woman, "I still say it's money."

"Goddamn what it is!" piped in a little man wearing an apron and carrying two dressed chickens wrapped in damp, blood-spotted burlap. "Why don't the bastard stop stallin' and jump?"

63

"Cause he ain't gonna," said the redhead. "If the suma-bitch was serious, he wouldn't a picked a busy street like this in broad daylight. There's too many other ways. Lots surer and lot less pain. He's bluffin' I tell ya. A goddamn phony."

The blond woman turned angrily, her shoddy coat swinging a heavy musk. "Why don' cha shut up! You don't know what the hell yer talking about. The poor slob's in real trouble and I say he's gonna fall right inta this lousy crowd."

"Bullshit!" The redheaded man shouted. "I say bullshit. And I'm laying twelve to five the phony bastard punks out— any takers?"

The fat blond was on him. "Yer got yerself a bet, mister!"

"Did I hear somebody say twelve to five?" A near voice inquired.

"Ya bet your sweet ass ya did!"

"Yeah, well you gotta bet, sucker!"

"Ya ain't said nothing, buster, I'll take somma that."

"Hey Dick, there's a chump over here laying twelve to five the bird won't fly offa his nest!"

"Wheeee! Hold him tight till I get over there!"

"Oh! You're all awful, awful! Why doesn't someone help that poor man? He looks so lonely up there. So lonely and scared." Chant. Chant. Clap. Clap. Clap.

A monotone produces varied effects. To Father Bloom, the steady hum of the elevator was another testament of the patience of our Lord towards man and his petty inventions: his things. That was the word Father Bloom utilized for any-thing not blessed with the Creator's Image: thing. He followed closely the low pitch of the motor, feeling the slow escalation of the cubicle. There was a somnolent peacefulness here in the windowless lift with just the hum and the clean-looking young officer. I must remember this mood, thought the priest. Remember it and perhaps write a short anecdote about it; something about the unchanging hum that praises and accompanies man's ascent without altering or interfering. Ah, yes, the moral could be useful and readily grasped by the younger members of the parish. This was the Father's constant concern and worry: he was losing the young people. They were deserting the Church; they were losing faith; wasting their spirit and energy in militant and sensual gratifications: dances, marches, sit-ins, protests, outrageous books, trashy shows. Faith was dissolving under a cloud of cobalt and hydrogen. Chemistry was becoming the Prophecy and politics the Testament. More and more, people were becoming things. Yes, this was indeed a worry to the erect, sprightly disciple.

He didn't like to think along the vein he was now thinking. It seemed, unjustly, to throw a shadow of doubt upon his faith in the Supreme Plan. Deep in his consciousness a question mark was faintly inked behind God's Will, and this caused him anguish beyond normal comprehension.

Father Bloom had doubted his faith only twice since his conversion. The last time had been in 1944, when his father, all three of his sisters, and their offspring, had been fed into the crematory. (The silence of His Holiness had almost destroyed him. But the Rock had withstood all.)

The first shock of fallibility, however, had been the worst.

Never would he forget the month of his graduation from the seminary, when because of his mother's illness he had returned home and for the first time faced his family as a Catholic. Clearly, he could still see that hated meeting; his father in the frayed yamulka standing proud and unspeaking, the Torah in his gnarled hand and Jehovah astride the bent shoulders; his sisters glaring dolefully as at a corpse; but beside them—and this the most painful memory of his life— his mother, gray and wasted, the mutant cells bursting and multiplying, eating away, devouring all strength and substance from the wracked body, taking one disgusted look at the stiff white collar and spitting on him. Spitting! Never would he forget the thick spittle shooting from the crumbling mouth, a few unbroken strands dribbling from her pale chin. And then the ultimate curse, the indictment that haunts still; the one gargled word that escaped his mother's dying slavering mouth. A word torn from the growing sore within her. "Dr–e–eck!" she had hissed wetly. All the hate and disgust of her diseased body sounded in that one word. Her fiery eyes elaborating for her failing throat. Garbage! screamed the eyes. Worthless scum of a corrupt seed! Vile unclean slime! Shit of my womb! Shit! Shit!

"Dreck!" she called him, and dreck he would be for all eternity.

For a moment, there in the warm droning elevator, Father Bloom's eyes watered. But he quickly shook the memory from his mind. I must remember to confess all of this tonight, he thought determinedly.

66

"Do you know if this man is of the Faith?" he asked the policeman beside him.

"Uh . . . no, sir . . . er, Father. Like I said, he only spoke that once, about his speaking English, and then he clammed up."

The Father nodded, keeping half of his mind on the humming. "I see, well, no matter," a slight smile tinged his lips, "we'll do whatever we can for the poor creature." He had almost said thing.

His tongue rasped teasingly across the cracked lower lip, pushing tiny blobs of coagulated blood into the wind. Manuel sighed at the salty taste of the stings. It was getting fainter, this sensation of pain here in the cold wind and darkening sky. Dimly, Manuel regretted not having the foresight to have chosen a ledge facing west. The sun would have preserved his blue that much longer. But small matter this, when one thought of all he had encompassed this bright autumn day.

A movement from the window caused him to stiffen and to push away from the wall!

"No! Don't be afraid, my son," Father Bloom cautioned, "you mustn't be afraid. I'm here to help."

The muscles of Manuel's neck were coiled for the spring of his jump. His small head swiveled stiffly to the window. There was an audible gasp from Manuel when he saw the priest.

Jutting from the starched, immaculately white collar was the most brutal face Manuel had ever seen. The small, dark eyes of the priest seemed without sockets, just stuck in the puffed red face like pinheads in an overboiled lump of meat. A shock of black canine hair sprouted like a straw wig from his offsided knobby head.

Father Bloom was fully aware of the impression he made on people the first time they saw him. What he didn't know about was the reserve of bitterness stored in the underside of his heart because of it. There was a light joke around the parish that Father Bloom was the only priest in the world who had to sneak up on a holy candle to avoid scaring the flame away.

Patiently, Father Bloom waited a few moments for the effect to wear off, or at least lose its shock potential, before he continued speaking: "I have come to help you, my son." Another pause, and then: "Are you of the faith, my son?"

Manuel blinked, achromatic figures flickered across the inner lids: his mother praying before revered icons . . .

Dios te salve, Maria, Llena eres de gracia; el Senor es contigo . . .

Precious bread money sizzling in the beeswax of the holy flame.

Y bendito es el fruto de tu vientre, Jesus . . . Santa Maria, Madre de Dios . . .

Hot guano-stenched beans, meal-mired and swimming in peppers left too long on the vine.

Bendicenos, Senor a nostros, y bendice . . . te damos gracias por todos . . . Omnipotente Dios . . .

Forgotten words entered him as embalming fluid enters a corpse rendering the veins forever alien to the bubbling of

68

life's blood. He saw them all vividly: mother, wife, daughters, sisters, the fragile lace-wrought shawls framing flat asiatic portraits. All making vague gestures of homage.

Y en Jesucristo su unico Hijo nuestro Senor que fue . . . del Espiritu Santo, y nacio de . . .

Manuel looked directly at the priest.

"No," he lied calmly, "I am not of your faith."

A brief look that could have been relief washed above the white collar and was gone. Manuel noticed it and smiled.

"Yes, Father, you are safe."

Father Bloom frowned, "Safe? I? No, my son, none of us are safe as long as one among us disdains the most precious gift of our blessed Savior!" He shook his head sadly and sighed, "How I wish that you *were* of the True Faith. My task would be far easier. As it now stands I must rely upon your ability to reason and your willingness to open your mind and heart to the incessant voice of the undying Spirit that is within us all."

The priest continued talking in a soothing voice. The calmness of his tone belied the tension he felt. Somehow, in that sense born of the supernatural, he knew that Manuel was lying, that here before him was a true prodigal of the Church. He felt—in some undefined, ecclesiastical way common to mystics—that this was a test of his faith.

The heavy cop leaned over the windowsill and whispered into Father Bloom's ear. The priest nodded without breaking his speech, then inquired casually:

"Is there anyone you would like to have summoned? Some

loved one you wish to have notified of your . . . your troubles?"

A sad look dropped over Manuel, "Yes," he answered.

The Father brightened. "Well, fine, if you will just—"

"She's dead," said Manuel, abruptly choking off the brightness.

"Dead?"

"Yes," replied Manuel calmly.

"Who's dead?" asked the priest.

"My wife, Ria," said Manuel as if drugged. "You see, Father, I killed her and the children this morning while they slept." Manuel leaned closer, relishing the shocked horror on the clergyman's face. "I cut their throats—my wife Ria, the girls, our little boy, all of them. I slit their throats and watched them die in the morning gloom."

Father Bloom, caught completely off guard, was stupefied. Agitated voices came from the hallway behind him; he waved them quiet.

"Would you . . . could I ask your name, my son?"

Manuel hesitated, then chuckled, reached into his pocket and shoved a greasy thin wallet along the ledge.

"What's the difference?" he said. "It's done and there's nothing you or anyone can do about it or . . ." he spoke emphatically, "because of it."

Father Bloom caught the wallet on the slide, scanned through it, and quickly passed it to someone in the hall behind him.

The tension of a moment earlier was now threefold. Oh, how sadly he had underestimated the test! Mortal sin at its worst—that's what he had sensed from the moment he entered the elevator. The Angel of Death himself was incarnate on this ledge! Father Bloom looked compassionately at Manuel. This poor creature, he thought, how can his layman's mind conceive of the darkness that has invaded him and seeks to steal yet another of the Lord's creatures? But it will not be an easy task, Evil One. No, we shall surely duel for this tainted soul! The Apostle's Legacy would not be wanting today.

"My son . . . Manuel," said the priest, "If you have committed the terrible deed that you have confessed to, then, there is a lot more at stake on this ledge than either of us had anticipated. I do not expect you to understand me completely, but you must trust me. As a start, you must forgive me if I don't believe you when you say that you are not of the True Faith. I sense in you the transcendent glow of one who has known Grace; of one who has been exposed to the Revelation and the Irrevocable Vow. I see here before me a man lost, in shadow, a tortured soul beaten and subjugated by evil, but who has not given up, has not cast out the Godhead from within; one who instead has climbed out here in front of the entire world to ask for—plead for—help in the eternal struggle."

The speech, delivered in a clear evangelistic voice of steel, shook Manuel. He stared suspiciously for a second or two, then burst out laughing.

Father Bloom, apparently unperturbed, continued:

"My son, you must realize that you have committed a Real Sin. But the fact that you are here at the edge of doom is proof of your remorse, your recognition and shame of the terrible act you have committed. But this," his head nodded to the crowd below, "is not the way. This merely compounds the already abominable sin. This shameful act wilfully refutes God's Will and damns you for eternity."

The wind blew colder. The crowd below seemed to grow distant, traveling on the rise and fall of the bell-like voice.

"No, Manuel, you must not do this thing. We must not give the devil his spoils. Instead we must fight him, defeat him! You are not lost, my son, not to our Divine Creator, our all merciful Father. We must do penance, confess, sacrifice; do good deeds and have good thoughts. We must prove our extreme regret at having offended His wishes."

Manuel's face grew more and more incredulous as the priest spoke. The laughter was gone and the skin around the full mouth was tight and disgusted.

"Regret? Penance? Sacrifice?" Manuel nearly choked. "What the hell are you talking about? I don't have any regret. I killed them because *I* decided it was best. Because it was what *I wanted* to do, just as *I want* to go off this ledge, not because—"

"No, Manuel! This is not true! It is not you speaking, but the evil that has taken possession of you. We must rid you of it. You have only to will it and that which is the ugliest, the most despicable in the sight of the Lord will be cast out!"

"Will you listen to me!" Manuel screamed, spittle spotting the corners of his mouth. "I don't want your damned Grace! Do you understand that? There's nothing wrong with me! I'm here out of preference. *I want to die*. Is that so difficult for your holy mind to bite on? I want only to be left alone and to die in my own way. I'm sick and tired of it all: the motion, the hypocrisy, the meaninglessness, the retrogression; all of it. There comes a time when one must decide not if one *wants* to live or die, but only if one *can* go on."

"One *must* go on, Manuel. It is God's Will. He has given us life and we belong to Him totally. We must bear our privations, our burdens, as the Christ bore the Crucifixion for us all. This is true heroism." Again the knobby head nodded downwards, "Suicide is a sinful cowardice."

Manuel frowned; he had expected something stronger than an old chestnut. A flush of superiority engulfed him.

"The great cry of Genus Homo," he scoffed, "only cowards kill themselves!"

"It is a truth, Manuel."

"It's a nothing! Believe me, Father, dying wilfully and by one's own hand is the most frightful, and consequently, most dangerous act open to Man. It is an act of magnificent magnitude when Man takes the life of man, but this transcends into divinity when Man takes the life of self."

"But Manuel, your family, your wife and children—"

"It was the only way, Father."

As Manuel was speaking, the young cop tried to squeeze on the ledge beside Father Bloom, but the window was much too narrow for the two of them and the priest angrily shushed the overzealous officer.

The connection broken, Manuel opportunely turned his attention back to the crowd. He searched the fringes of the crowd for the young girl he had cursed earlier, but she had

73

either gone or moved deeper within the crowd. This bothered Manuel for some shapeless reason and for a few seconds he searched frantically, but vainly, for the bright spot of yellow. Dimly, he heard the Priest's voice rising, return to contention. Too late, Padre, too late. The line is dead.

Eight floors below:

"Aw, c'mon. This bum ain't gonna jump."

"I dunno, he might. He's been out there a long time now."

"Yeah, that's what I mean. Too long. Besides, I'm starving and in case you forgot, the girls are waiting for us to buy 'em lunch."

"Sure, sure, I know, but we been here all this time, another few minutes won't hurt. I think the sumbitch's 'bout ready to go."

"What're you, some kinda jump freak or sumpin? The hell with this creep. Let's go. It's just round the corner."

"Yeah, well you go ahead, huh? Order me the corned beef special and tell the girls I'll be there right away."

"What're you kidding me, or sumping? C'mon!"

"Look, I'll be there in a minute. Now, stop buggin' me, ha? I ain't stood here this long for nothing. If that sumbitch jumps I gonna see it!"

". . . even the governing authorities, representing God, are allowed—only as a reprehensible and final resort—to inflict . . ."

The words wrapped around the priest's bulky presence

droned out of the void, gently nudging Manuel back to the ledge,

". . . no man has the right to decide whether or not he chooses to live or die; not for himself and most certainly not for others—"

"No right?" yelled Manuel, angrily back on the ledge, "I have the *only* right! I am not awed by the unknown, not paralyzed by fear, yes Father, fear, fear of some mythical burning hell."

Father Bloom's eyes flashed their first sign of anger. "No, Manuel, not fear! Never fear! Love—love of the Creator, and sorrow for man's original sin. Remorse for being far less than He had designed us to be in His supreme plan. Love, Manuel, love! But never enough, never a balance. Man at his utmost can give only a finite response to God's infinite love for His creatures."

Manuel shivered. Without warning the air was crystal frigid.

". . . an offense Manuel, you have wilfully offended God's wishes, and—"

"Offended God's wishes?" Manuel's voice was derisive. "Who are you to dictate God's wishes to me?"

Father Bloom drew himself up proudly, " 'Do this unto me,' Christ said unto the Apostles, 'In the name of the Father, and of the Son, and the Holy Ghost, teach them all that I have commanded you!' These were the words of the first Communion. And Saint Peter has so commissioned for all eternity."

ARNOLD KEMP

"I see," said Manuel, "I suppose that means Peter never needed to wipe his ass."

"Manuel!"

Father Bloom was stunned by the blasphemy. He stared in pain, distraught more at his own error than Manuel's heresy.

I was wrong, he thought, he is not of the Faith. I have blundered. I have argued faith with a man who denies not only the Image but the Light that casts it.

Father Bloom was dejected. His dejection so abject that Manuel was touched. There was a gentleness in Manuel's voice when he spoke, the words barely riding over the crowd and the wind:

"Please, do not despair."

Surprise showed on Father Bloom's face at Manuel's gentleness.

"I only believe in the freedom to live as I see fit. Freedom to slake my darkest urge. Limitless freedom."

"Freedom doesn't mean the right to destroy!"

"Wrong again, Father. The right to destroy is the *only* freedom. And rapidly becoming the only pleasure."

Manuel raised his nose and sniffed the cold air. He wondered if later the blue would be all gone.

The priest, too, was strangely silent, his eyes also surveying the sky.

Without looking at him, Manuel said very softly:

"I have concluded that what you and your ilk have been preaching for centuries is undoubtedly correct—man must obviously die before he can obtain life."

*   *   *

76

The crowd had grown. Tripled. Housewives forgot their shopping. Workers stretched their scant lunch hour, then said the hell with it and took the afternoon. Old ladies, little boys, tourists, pickpockets, they all watched and waited for the fool on the ledge to jump. They climbed over the gleaming fire engines and squat police cars; they jostled the sawhorse police barriers and bravely baited the uniformed rescuers with barbs of salt. It was carnival! Abandon! A day in the sun! Russian roulette with a mannequin's head and marshmallow bullets. Escape from the cowboys, doctors, and maddening soap commercials wait at home and office. Oogly boobly, chew muuchi muuchi gum. Frappi pappi mappi, brush with akalakie. Hotcha potcha, eat our tomatchi. Not today. Not today. Today was adventure. Today was drama. That idiot, that madman up there might, just might, jump. I might see him splatter. I might hear the crunch. A drop of blood might splatter my sleeve. Oh, Christ, wouldn't that be something to show Marge and the kids tonight! He might, he might. He just might.

A group of young undergraduates with matched sweaters began to cap in unison, their collective voices uttering a single guttural chant: "Jump, jump, jump, jump!" One of the young men leaped to the top of a parked car, threw up both hands, yelled, and made a playful leap to his friends who caught him amid wild laughter and applause from the immediate crowd. The chant was picked up, the clapping became louder, more heated: "Jump, jump, jump, jump!"

A line of boys and girls, high school students passing through on a school trip, stopped to ogle and jeer. Their teacher, a mild young black woman with glasses and bobbed hair, tried to usher them on, cajoling and admonishing them until a burly, pimple-faced boy with honey hair stepped out of line and exploded a vicious fist in the middle of her face, smashing lip, nose and glasses. She fell, a meaty slab, and lay still; her students began to dance around her, kicking and stomping the inert body in time to their own primitive chant: "Yeah, yeah, yeah, kick, yeah, yeah, kick!"

A saxophone appeared and suddenly the car fenders were bongos, tambalies, congas, drums of all types and pitches. Sedate office girls in tight skirts began to shimmy and stamp. The shrill cry ripping dainty tongues from steamed, watering mouths: "Jump, jump, jump, yeah, yeah, kick, jump, jump, jump!"

The spiraling iridescence of sky and color had so dazzled Manuel that the crowd was a wiggling blob, a blur that his weakening eyes fought to bring into focus.

The crowd's chanting captivated Manuel. His head swirled with the cadence: jump, jump, clap, clap, jump, jump. Manuel laughed, threw his head back with abandonment. Ah, God, this felt good! He no longer hated them. He laughed and clapped, swinging his hanging feet, waved to the crowd. They ate it up! The crowd loved it! They were with him. This was the spirit! The American way! Jump. Jump. Jump. Jump.

Father Bloom yelled above the crowd and the wind, pleading for recognition. From the hallway a strong insistent voice began shouting for the priest. Reluctantly, Father

Bloom turned and stuck his red artificial face into the window for a quick instant. When he re-emerged the flush was gone, his face now a doughy pale lump.

"Manuel! Manuel, listen to me!" Father Bloom yelled, beckoning with his free hand.

The motion caused Manuel to turn his grinning head towards the priest.

"Manuel," Father Bloom said slowly, distinctly, "We have just this moment contacted your wife Ria. Do you hear me? We have just finished talking to your wife on the phone. She isn't dead, Manuel! She's fine and so are your children! It seems you've been missing for two days and they're worried about you, but other than that they're well and healthy. Do you understand me? You've imagined it all. Your family is fine! Your wife is on her way here now. Manuel? Do you understand what I'm saying, Manuel?"

The priest's pink lips sliced the air like tiny scimitars. Manuel continued to clap, grinning and bobbing his head in time with the crowd's rhythm. There was meaning to nothing. Nothing except the rising throbbing beat. Clap, clap, clap, ". . . two days Manuel . . . worried to death . . . police . . ." Clap. " . . . here, now . . . delusions . . . need help . . . figment . . ." Clap, clap. " . . . here my son, grasp my hand. Come let us get in out of the cold and wait for your wife."

Father Bloom crawled completely out on the ledge, only the ankle of one leg remained hooked to the windowsill. "Here, Manuel, my hand!"

The bony hand loomed at Manuel from a dark, frayed sleeve. For an indecisive second or two Manuel merely stared at the sleeve, then hesitantly, began to push his own right hand forward along the ledge, his left hand keeping time on his hopping thigh: chant, chant, plop, plop, plop.

It was a painful stretch for Father Bloom and little moisture balls beaded his forehead. Slowly, slowly, stretch, a little further. Their fingers touched! Paper-dry palms fronted and slid snugly onto pulsating wrists. Both grips locked. Their eyes met. Father Bloom grinned. Manuel grinned wider. I've done it! thought the priest proudly. I've saved him for you, Father.

"D'TZACH, ADASH, B'AHAB!"

The words thundered through Father Bloom, withering his neck beneath the bright collar.

D'tzach, Adash, B'ahab! Blood and boils! Creeping vermin! Locusts swarming out of yellow-green darkness! The first born! The first born! Father Bloom looked down and saw his mother, circulating in the crowd below. She looked at him, and her rotting lips puckered for speech, for the *word.* Father Bloom twisted on the ledge, croaking sounds damming his shrunken throat.

"Dreck!" she called him. Again, the horrid indictment splashing like fire. "Dreck!" sounded his mother's lips.

He yanked at his arm, wanting to ward off the sound. There was no release, Manuel held fast.

"Shit!" screamed the daughter of Abraham.

Father Bloom cringed as if his spine had been crushed. Above it all he could hear the wild whooping laughter of Manuel.

The priest knew.

There was one clear painless moment of prescience. One

wet blink of lashes to feel the unyielding grip on his wrist tighten.

"Shit!"

Manuel jumped.

"Goddammit, give us some help up here!" screamed the swarthy policeman.

The two policemen scrambled in the narrow window, tugging at the priest's trousers. They had a dubious grip on one shoeless foot, having lost the shoe, and almost the priest, at the first vicious jerk.

"Pull, goddammit!"

"I can't, that crazy bastard's still got ahold of him!"

"Pull, dammit, pull!"

They leaned, fighting, unable to work effectively in the small opening. Father Bloom's pants gave suddenly, the belt snapping apart, sending buttons and buckle flying like small planets shot from orbit.

"Look out!" yelled the young cop, "His pants are coming apart!"

"Hell with his pants," yelled his partner. "The leg, get the other leg!"

They dangled in a sick parody of a slapstick film. The two hatless policemen bumbling over one another in the window, trying to hold onto the priest while his pants slowly disintegrated. The priest himself upside down, spreadeagled, one foot flapping in the wind like a spasmodic beacon. And the last link of the comic chain: Manuel. The Madman.

Manuel was quite calm. His dark eyes sunken hollows in

the deep recesses of the high, bony cheekbones. A grin was locked on his face grimly, for all time. He didn't move. Didn't pull, or twist, or turn, just hung there grinning up into Father Bloom's convulsing features. The insanity in the priest's face delighted Manuel. The priest had lost touch completely. He made weird gibbering sounds, a babble of English, Latin, Yiddish, Hebrew; strange Eastern sounds mixed with a constant mewing whine. Thick slobber dribbled from his slack mouth and stained the hanging collar. The collar itself had torn loose in the first shock of the fall and now streamed with the wind, catching yellow mucus from the quivering chin and fanning it into the currents.

Nothing has changed, thought Manuel serenely, nothing. The sky has seemingly darkened to a near-purple, but that's only a trick of eye and light. The blue is still there. They can't fool me any more. I've caught on to all their sneaky illusions.

The arm connecting him to the priest was no longer burning, it had slowly cooled, thin needles of ice prickling the skin; it, too, was now apart from him. Manuel tried to bring his left arm up to bolster the numbing right one, but he couldn't manage it. All of his strength was leaving him, the body-juices draining upwards. A thin white vapor drifted between his face and the priest's. Manuel fought to see through it, desperately squinting and straining to keep the man's head framed in the deepening blue.

Shhoooooopp!

The Father left him! Shot away with a deafening roar! Manuel screamed at him to come back. Come back, you bastard! Come back! But it was no use. The roar was too great, the distance too far. Helplessly, he watched the priest's face grow smaller and smaller, merging with the blue, until it struck like a stone strikes calm waters, casting a single breaking ripple that folded over the roar and covered the universe with a warm black peace.

AUDREY M. LEE

Waiting for Her Train

She sits in Thirtieth Street Station watching the newsman over the three-screen television. She is waiting for her train to come in. The station vibrates with arrival and departure of trains. Hers does not arrive. But she has time. Other people are waiting, too. Expectant. Anxious. They have schedules to meet. Destinations. They have purchased tickets—round trip or one-way. She has not purchased her ticket yet. A ticket represents a destination. She has not decided upon her destination. But who is to know . . .

She recognizes the old woman wearing two dresses and two sweaters and carrying the shopping bag full of her possessions. She will not be as obvious as the old lady. There will never be a vagrant look about her. She has locked her possessions in one of the station lockers. Her presence in the station is temporary—just until her train comes in. And for all anyone knows, her baggage is being shipped ahead of her. She is waiting for her train no matter *what* anyone might think.

The railroad workers for the day shift are coming into the station. They are looking at her as usual. They think they know but they don't. Those tolerant looks that express knowing—as if she were a distant relative in their house. A poor distant relative who has had a bad stroke of luck. What of it? She has had a taste of the finer things. She has been to the Art Museum, stood among the Picassos and the Powells —and oh too many paintings to be mentioned. The fact remains that she has been. She knows something about fashion, too. About designing. About labels—labels tell so much about quality. And they lend respectability to clothing. She has no proof that she knows, except the dress she is wearing. Her creditors have reclaimed all the others, along with the shoes. They were right, of course. But they couldn't deny she had discriminating taste. But that is behind her. She must look to the future.

At eight o'clock the Horn and Hardart Restaurant will open. She will go there as usual. And afterwards—well, she would see.

"North Philadelphia. Trenton. Princeton. Newark. New York. Now loading on platform number three."

Not her train. She is waiting for something more exotic. A tropic island with palm trees. There are so many people going places. And so many people returning. She likes this time of morning. Her train would come in the morning. It would pull into the station on velvet springs. And it would purr, not screech. Her man would be waiting with her bags.

And she would be clothed in quiet elegance, the labels of the day's fashion turned in, reassuring against her skin, the quality turned out for everyone to see. That would teach the know-alls. The railroad workers who passed her bench, throwing their tolerant glances. That would prove that she had been waiting for her train after all. That she was going somewhere.

Horn and Hardart opens. She gets up from the bench, brushes the wrinkles that resist her pressure. When she bought the dress it was wrinkle-resistant. She puts on her soiled gloves and respectable walk, feeling the kinks loosen in her knees, giving them a jerk or two when no one is looking. She picks up a newspaper from a bench. Someone is always leaving a newspaper. Then she checks the return coin slots of the telephones. No forgotten dimes. She will not have coffee this morning.

Inside Horn and Hardart, she is reading the specials posted on the menu. Later on breakfast will cost more. She is giving the menu a respectable glance, demonstrating her discriminating taste with proper deliberation. Then with the same deliberating eye, she looks at the long line of people waiting to take advantage of the early morning special breakfasts. A glass of water will do until the line is shorter. That is her reasoning. She tugs decisively at her glove and fills her glass with cool water from the fountain and sits down to a table near the window to read the newspaper. But first she will make the table ready for breakfast. She lays knife, fork and spoon, the napkin. There.

The newspaper. She will choose a supermarket to visit

from those advertised. She wonders how many different supermarkets she has shopped in over the past.

Nine o'clock. She is entering the supermarket. She fills her cart with steaks, chops, parsley, fruit. She will eat an orange while she shops. Cheese—she would taste a piece of cheese, too. Not the same brand she had yesterday at the other market. This cheese is sharper. Raisin bread. She will eat a slice or two.

She opens a jar of herring. Herring for breakfast—oh well, one eats what one finds convenient. Besides, fish is a necessary part of the diet, too. The manager is smiling and handing her glove to her.

"Looks like you're having your breakfast . . ."

Kidding her, of course. People are always chewing on something when they go to market. "Yes. You have good herring." The compliment pleases him. "Very good herring," she is saying for emphasis. He is smiling and walking away.

Bananas—bananas are filling. She needs something that will fill her. Meanwhile, she must appear in earnest. She must fill her cart with household articles. A mop handle and mop. That would look impressive jutting from the cart. There—now another bite of banana. Paper napkins from the shelf. Table salt. Black pepper. Paprika . . .

She swallows the last of the banana. Then she puts on her gloves, pushes the cartful of groceries to the front of the store, places it in a respectful position just to one side of the checkout counter, out of the path of shoppers waiting in line for the cashier. And in a respectable voice:

"Cashier—I forgot my purse—I wonder if you would be kind enough to let my cart stay here until I return . . .

"Certainly, madam."

"I appreciate it. Thanks so much." She burps. Bananas take a while to digest. But she has time. She hurries from the market. She does not want the manager to see her leaving. He might suggest sending the groceries to her—sweet of him, of course—but how could she explain—what could she say—that she was waiting for a train? Well, she had escaped now. Explanations are not necessary.

In D-D's Department Store she stands before the cosmetics counter, trying on a sample lipstick. She doesn't like it well enough to buy it. She tries the expensive face power which the saleslady mixes for her. A spoonful of white power. A spoonful of pinkish power, mint-colored power. Then blending them with a spatula.

"You look absolutely gorgeous—this is wonderful and it's good for your skin. Put this on and wipe it dry—work that in—truly pink would be equal to your natural—"

"I was looking for something quick and easy. I don't have time to do much in the morning . . ."

"Try this," dipping the spoon into the powder. Wiping the spoon and dipping it into another powder. "This has orange in it. You have to use it sparingly—you need some color—it's a sample portion. Try it out at home—try them both—and see how you like them."

"Thank you very much. Maybe I can come back tomorrow —if I decide I like the way it looks on me. These lights—if I were only at home . . .

"You'll like it."

One mirror is seldom true. One has to consider the majority of mirrors. She smiles at the woman. Then she walks toward the perfumes. Aura of Emotion—Charles of the Ritz —Desert Flower—Desert Flower is too incongruous a name to be considered by a bench sitter. Still she must try something new. Yesterday it was Heaven Scent. Today—well— it would depend—Chantilly—she felt like *Chantilly*—but first . . . She looked at the bottles of perfume and toilet water, picked them up, read their labels. She is a discriminating shopper. All the bottles scrutinized. She picks up the spray bottle of Chantilly. Poof—savors the scent with a sensitive and discriminating nose. That is what she wants. She sprays her ears, wrists, clothing. All very quickly and tastefully. Subtly. She wants to be sure of catching the scent.

"It smells good. May I show you something, madam? We have the talcum, too. It will make a nice set . . ."

She is very discriminating, so she will not answer right away. She has not made up her mind—not really—Chanel No. 5. Intimate.

"Excuse me a minute, madam. I'll wait on this customer— I know you want to take your time—when you decide . . ."

Poof. Chantilly behind her ears once more. Subtly. Discriminatingly. The saleslady is busy. Several customers are waiting. She pulls her gloves securely over her hands, resumes her respectable posture and walks out of the store. The scent does indeed smell good on. Now she will return to the station and wash her gloves. She will lay them on the bench to dry. If only she had a portable hair dryer, she could wash her hair. But portable hair dryers are made for people of means—not for people of predicament.

Back at the station powder room. She washes her gloves, touches her hair, and checks her makeup. The powder goes well with her complexion. And so does the lipstick. She checks her purse, making certain she still has the samples in her purse, touches her hair again, approves. Still she would like to get her hair washed and styled. She will think of a way. But having the new makeup and the perfume makes her feel somewhat refreshed. She will settle down on a bench to watch the pictures, plan the dinner menu, decided upon the evening's entertainment.

And of course, she will watch the evening flow of men and women in and out of the station. But before that, she will check the coin return slots of the telephones. Nothing yet. She will have to wait for her coffee a little longer. The best time to check the slots is just after the rush hour. She might even be able to afford two cups of coffee. And who is there to deny that her train might have arrived by then.

JOHN McCLUSKEY

The Pilgrims

Steel girders reach three stories for the sky. Two floors on the building have already been completed and that's where most of the brothers are now, cleaning up, setting up, cutting up. I'm told that it will be an office building with no windows, just peepholes to keep an eye on the natives. Here in the middle of their turf. Battalions of blonde secretaries will be bussed in and men handcuffed to attaché cases will be shot through tubes that run clear to their front doors in NeverNigger Land. If I didn't need the job so bad I'd help burn it down. Or throw a brick. Or, at least picket, like the welfare mother and the nationalist brother behind me. As it has turned out I didn't look them in their eyes when I came an hour ago. Shame, their eyes must have warned. Is a steak more important than your dignity? When you're down to peanut butter and crackers, dignity is an old souvenir you hock and feel no pain. They watch me even now, hoping I will get hip and break from the little fire, the brooding Puerto Rican, the two Italians and the two brothers who rap to kill the cold.

This idea has been Wendell's more than mine. Wendell is the elegant fag who lives next door. Later this morning he'll be auditioning for a part in a play he doesn't like and he will get the job because he has told me he will. We've agreed that I am in bad bad shape. We've agreed that I'm not above robbing or killing to keep from starving. Like any man. I have had enough of sudsbusting at the cafeteria. The Post Office is two weeks of changes just getting hired and the hospitals aren't hiring now. So I hang around construction sites. Wendell's friends have told him that construction work will be about the best and quickest money. My running buddy Ubangi and his buddies have said it's for chumps with no mind. None of them have told me that it's a risk getting on, especially in the dead of winter when work is slowest and the crews are smallest. The work whistle has blown ten minutes ago and still I'm sitting with no promise of anything. Nothing except off-the-wall conversation and all the morning air I can swallow.

"Fire more important, Swine," says the skinny man. "If they wasn't no fire, you'd be eating meat raw like white folks do and if they wasn't no fire you'd be freezing your narrow ass off right now. And don't try to tell me no different."

The brother called Swine scratches his double chin and laughs. "My mama told me a long time ago not to ever try to tell a fool anything. But all this time I done figured you just half a fool, King. And I say that to say that you might

94

half understand what I'm saying. If there wasn't no water, you woulda dried up in your mama's belly and not be here to argue about which is more important."

"Don't talk about my mama! I don't play that shit."

"Shut up, fool! Ain't nobody studyin' you or your mama neither. If a bird had your brains, he'd fly backwards, I swear."

King warms his rustydusty hands over the fire, then passes on a skin magazine that the Italians have been grinning over. You got your nerve talking about somebody being dumb when you about as heavy as one of them snowflakes yonder . . ."

Across the street the snow sticks to the trash piled high in cans squatting at the curb. Damn all of it. Wendell, the cold, my empty pockets, the hard can I'm sitting on and now the snow. Damn it all. Every musician in this town can't be starving. And I *know* I'm bad. Quiet as it's kept I know I'm about the baddest around. I know I'm bad. Even if nobody else knows.

Suddenly the foreman like an ugly hope over us. He looks directly at each of us. Again. His mouth working to shoot out tobacco juice and his eyes settling on the Italians.

"You two follow me!" And off they go into the bottom floor.

"Damn Whitey a bitch, ain't he? He knew who he was gone pick when he first got over here. Always looking out for number one. More bloods gone have to think that way more often."

95

"When we get something," says King. "Them's that got keep on gettin'."

Bent into the wind, junkies nod past. There have been other winds and darker days when I have whistled tunes over the growling in my belly. Columbus, Ohio, for example. Columbus looked a lot like Kansas City to me. Settled and closed. Columbus, where bloods loved their old Buicks and where I hung out afternoons in a poolhall and talked trash and watched foundry workers make it to the liquor store after work. A pimp town they called it, those who couldn't get away. A pimp town because of the popcorn pimps standing alone on corners going hungry. Then a job in a foundry came my way and I sweated and settled and wondered if I would ever get away. Days I worked alongside dirtyhaired hillbillies who left Kentucky to die in the shadow of factories. Nights I looked for work playing my horn.

Two months into town came the night I really got going. The eagle had swooped that day and Cecil, a skinny dude with a beard who worked the same shift with me, pulled my coat to the Blue Gardenia Club.

"Bring you ax down tonight and, like, sit in with us. Sometimes we get some sessions with cats coming up and sitting in. But then again we get a lot of cats who come on like a hurricane and go out pooting. You never know." So I bought a box of reeds, a new pair of bellbottoms, and called myself ready.

After two numbers the house was on fire. Drunks paid attention and the waitresses stopped waiting. The best man on the stand was Snooky, the organist, just one year out of

Macon, Georgia. He chased me onto another track, a track that led through the secret fires of all those listening. They danced between the tables and at the bar. Between sets, Snooky, shy Snooky, who never looked at you long, said: "In this town you don't hear shit that good every night." We slapped palms and he invited me to a party he was throwing for his sister that night.

"Run, muthfucka, run!" Two ripoffs in trenchcoats and big hats skidding across the street. One of them has a bag of money and coins are running everywhere, down his leg, everywhere. They must have skipped the bills to get the quarters. Cupcakes spilled out of inside pockets when they dipped to sweep up the change. Quarters as diamonds, cupcakes as gold. On the case, a siren is screaming just a few blocks away.

"Come on, man!" They shoot down the sidewalk and, in full stride, cut a right angle turn into an alley.

"Look at them jokers fly!" His trash cart parked, an old man has peeped it all. A woman carrying a shopping bag and cane has peeped him peeping. So when the coast looks clear they get to the coins about the same time, the woman leaning her cane against a fireplug. By the time the cops get there, they have blended back into the scenery. The first mistake the cops make is to pick on a helpless junkie sliding past.

"Get yo' hands off me, funky muthafuckin' pig muthafuckas!," screams the junkie, cooling his nod.

A bald man is jumping around the back seat of the cruiser

97

like a monkey trying to sit on a fire. He sticks his head out of the window and yells something at the cops. They yell something back and he pulls his head back in momentarily, moving all the while. The cops are bothering everybody on the block. No one has seen or heard anything. The pickets are especially blind.

"Is you crazy?" the welfare mother asks the cop who has crossed the street. "You gone come over here and ask me what I seen? You must be a fool. I wouldn't tell you bastards if I did know which way they went."

"Look, lady," I can hear him say, "this is important. They have just robbed a delicatessen of twenty dollars and we can take you downtown, you know, for withholding . . ."

And the picket sign is suddenly an axe after the necks of all the sergeant-at-arms who have messed up. It misses. Before you can say "up 'ginst the wall," the cop has drawn his club and is standing his ground, his lips curled like an Irish wolfhound's tasting battle.

"Y'all just keep fucking with us. Get on back where you belong. Get away from here!" And she charges toward the cop. The little nationalist is a blur. He catches her in front and stops her dead in her tracks. If I didn't see it, I wouldn't have believed it. He's outweighed by at least a hundred pounds and he stops her cold. She's stunned. She backs off a little and listens to the brother. Now is not the time, he is calmly saying. Now is not the time. The cop should thank him or something. After all, that woman might have taken the club and beaten him to a pulp. Then beat the pulp. But the cop just shakes his head and swaggers back to the car.

"See that?" I ask Swine and King who have stopped running their mouths. "See that?"

"What?"

"That little cat stop that woman? She was about to catch the cop with a sucker punch and you missed it."

"Yeah, but she a rough one, ain't she?" chuckles King. "A big woman like that don't be shucking if she moving that fast."

"I got one like that at home," says Swine, stroking his belly. "And she definitely ain't nothing to play with. And jealous? Man, you ain't seen nothing. Sometimes I tell her she got that graveyard love because she'd rather see me in the graveyard than with another woman. That's one reason I done stuck so close to home all these years."

"Ugly nigga like you can't pick up much in the street no way. It's best you housebound."

The ripoffs are blocks away now. Maybe they've ducked into a restaurant, and with alibis intact, have begun pouring Alaga syrup over hotcakes. Things on the street are already back to normal: junkies pushing on toward the magic touch, the trash man after his diamonds and the old woman to a quiet place. Maybe.

"Snooky's sister, man, is-wow-like how can I describe her? She is so fine like-wow-what can I say?" The man has been babbling like that ever since we left the club.

They called him Killer Joe, after the song, and he drove a Cadillac that smelled new. He knew everyone around the club and bought a lot of drinks for his special friends. The band, of course, was special and we'd get first word on the many parties he'd know about. People were hard on Killer. I always thought it was because he wasn't a hustler or anything they might fear. So they rode him heavy about the jailbait he'd be seen driving around every afternoon.

"You'll see her soon, my man. You'll see her."

Party-party people had packed the place. Some disguised as Indians, other as British lords, but most as the hip captives they were. Popping their fingers or just leaning back into the dark, smoking. Fine black women everywhere. My nose led me to the kitchen where bookoos liquor bottles sat on the table. After hiding one bottle, I reminded myself to pace the drinking. It had gotten so bad sometime before, that cats at the foundry had started calling me Cutty Sark.

"There the bitch is now!" That hotbreathing Killer Joe, slavering on me.

I moved to the edge of the crowd, trying to avoid Killer Joe. After all, I didn't need him or anyone else to point out Sassie Mae. If she was so bad, I'd know.

I began to wonder if I would leave the party alone and then there she was in front of me. There. I would know her but could not believe her fineness that made the room, the fingerpoppers, and the music nothing. She had just finished a dance and had turned to smile at me.

"You must be Mack. Don't look surprised. You see, I know every one else here. Snooky's already told me about you."

"I hope everything he's told you works in my favor."

"Well, that might depend on you."

I couldn't know then that the best thing I could have done

after that first dance with her would have been to run for the door. The frown at my questions, the way she held her head—all of it said something that I later called a warning. I wanted to listen, to hold her and listen, but she was soft as doctor's cotton and my feet forgot to move.

Killer Joe like a sudden shadow. "You got the hammer, Mack! You lucky nigga you. You got her!"

Later there were afternoons of heavy snows. Sassie Mae in the window of the record shop where she worked, fly Mae spinning oldies-but-goodies that were blasted over the street while she checked her makeup and her stockings in the mirrors. Knees and thighs on view to Mt. Vernon Street. Mae taking time out to help make time. Her winning the Saturday night Miss Miniskirt contest four times in a row and the prize wig she wore. Her walk wicked in every which way. Me, fumbling and there to stutter and watch her move to the stacks to the record player to the cash register. The quick kisses stolen on the sly. She, all four women of Simone. And more.

Boss Mae: "Mack, remember I'm a grown woman and I don't need nobody in this world to take care of me. Nobody. Not even Snooky. Don't start acting funny on me and try to keep giving me orders. We split the rent, we split the bills. You my man. You been my man for two months now, but don't start acting funny."

(The night she came in drunk after a big night out with the girls, a little club of single and bored schoolteachers she had started running with. I called them the Jive Five.)

Mouthrunning Mae: "And why don't you clean yourself

up sometime? Henrietta and Lucy be over here and you just be sitting up in your dirty workclothes belching beer like you don't know better and playing them dumb records over and over."

(Mingus mystified her, though Monk made her smile.)

Sweet Mae: "Do I ever ask you to do what I know no man can do? I've never asked you to pull down the moon and make it my diamond like some women will. I've never asked you to be king of anything. Just be a man. That's what any woman who calls herself a woman wants. Give only what you can. That's me, sugar. I can't help it, but that's me."

High Society Mae: "Look, Mack, I'm giving you slack and you just don't know it. I work. I got some money. I'm not like the others you see lying up in bed all day, curlers all in their hair. And, shit, I don't have to go around looking tacky either, fine as I am."

(A new dress thumbed to her shoulders and she whirled in the mirror, laughing in my angry face.)

I knew so much then and understood so little. Moving in together was a small decision and she had even begun suggesting marriage. That was too many changes away.

There were days when I walked around with my horn and pretended to look for jam sessions. Those days I ate greasy food and drank wine with strangers. Cold, I would tell myself, so cold she'd throw water on a drowning man. I had gone looking for a woman and came back with a child who mistook kindness for weakness. So we battled hard and long to stay real for one another.

(Bitch, you ain't the Queen of Sheba. I know we got bills

to pay but some nights I just like to lay here in the crib, you know? If your friends don't go for it, let the door catch them on their asses.)

I had been away for two days and suddenly started for the apartment, crashing the sidewalk games of children, running, past the conversations of thieves, running back to that biglegged woman of mine, bursting through the door.

"Sassie Mae!"

Mae, curled on the couch, eating an apple and reading *Jet* magazine. Her lips managing to mouth a few last lines before she looked up. "Nigga, you look like you on your last go 'round. Your other woman must not be doing you no good. Go take a bath and get yourself together. And another thing. The next time you make up your mind to go away and stay so long, don't expect me here when you get back."

"My love just came down on me a few minutes ago over by the park."

"If you got to leave me for two days to get your love to come down, then maybe we ought to hang it up now."

But she was fronting. She had been balling some herself. I could tell. Dirty dishes stacked in the sink and the dust an inch thick. Cigarette butts with lipstick traces, cigars—I could tell. Yeah, Mae, where are you sleeping this cold morning and whose breakfast will you be too sleepy to cook? Where do your sad lovers go to forget?

When the group got the contracts back, it was like an answer to all our prayers. Two club dates and two dances around the state. The dances were Snooky's idea. Weird

Snooky. Funky American Legion halls in small towns would
be soul injections, he claimed. The overhaul we needed.

"Y'all ain't been that long from these get-down dances that
y'all done forgot how to get over," he would say. "Mack, you
ain't forgot to honk, have you?"

"No, Snook. I ain't. But why should I go back to it?"

"It'll show you how far you've come," he said in his mystic's
voice. Cecil believed that the dude was simply homesick.
("That's all. We should chip in and buy him a bus ticket
to Macon and save ourselves all these changes.")

"Snooky, what do we get when we win this so-called Battle
of the Bands?" We had just pulled into the last town and
had found the dance hall.

"One hundred and fifty dollars apiece and a pat on the
back," he said.

"What if we lose?"

"Just the money," he grinned.

I made up my mind that I'd be so bad that night I'd have
the pimps dancing. I might even get so happy I'd sing "I've
Got a Woman" the way I did in Cleveland. Biscuit Brown
and the Untouchables were our competition. Sisters hung
close to the stage in Saturday night Afros and I slowdanced
with them while the Untouchables made noise or stood
around on the stage looking ugly. The sisters swore they
knew Columbus like the steps to the latest dances. Some
claimed they had heard me play there and one thought she
had two of my albums. I let her believe that and asked her
about her boyfriend watching us dance. They all had Mae's
voice, if not her hips, if not her perfume, if not her softness.

"I see you gone spend your money buying up all the pussy in this town," said the signifying Spooky.

"The night I have to buy pussy is the night the sun comes out."

Though most of the strays were taken up, I did find one for Snooky. She said she'd mess up his mind and keep him in that town for days.

Both bands were on stage for the last hour of the show. We alternated tunes and on one song I layed a lush line and a student of black music stuck in that town asked if I had ever heard of Gene Ammons. We chased the Untouchables off the stage, blew them into bad health. Any fool could have seen how close we were that night. I bent notes out of shape and Snooky built stairways right out to the night. We couldn't feel bad about losing. We knew the game. The locals needed the encouragement. After all, we had liked the crowd and the mommas who snapped their fingers and shimmied and made us welcome. We forgot the push and shove of our lives and found ourselves holding the hands of women whose faces we'd forget in two days. It was the night that was important, wasn't it? But wasn't it a mess in that overheated motel room with those large thighs wrapped tight around you, when you felt the first slipping away inside you and you whispered "Mae" and coughed until you re-membered the strange woman's name?

"Uh-huh, yeah," grunts King. "She plenty fine all right." He passes the picture on to Swine. After Swine has passed around his family picture, the least I can do is to show them the wrinkled snapshot of Sassie Mae I've kept in my wallet.

"A woman that fine can mean trouble," Swine says, passing the picture on to the Puerto Rican. "Was she?"

"Not at all, man."

"That's good," King says. "Bad women is my weakness. If I had brains for every bad woman I've had, I'd be running this world . . ."

"And be hard as hell on women."

"And be hard as hell on women. Say, brotherman, how long you been in this town?"

"One month," I tell him.

"Well, that's one month too long if you ask me. I been here fifteen years and you see where I'm at, don't you? Bad women, no money, and rednecks. Them's my downfall."

"Stop crying," complains Swine. He points at me. "This man here ain't got time to listen to you cry."

On their way to school, kids throw cans at a three-legged dog. The patrol car is still circling the block with the bald-headed monkey in back, scratching his nose. They must expect the ripoffs to come back for the few coins left on the sidewalk. Instead the kids scoop them up. The pickets laugh, Swine and King laugh, the Puerto Rican laughs. The harshness of this winter in the laughs.

The foreman hasn't looked our way for fifteen minutes. A bad sign, they say. All of us agree to shiver through another fifteen minutes. You never know what might pop up at the last minute.

THOMAS MULLER-THYM

A Word about Justice

The noon sun covered the asphalt schoolyard and caught Clyde in the middle of his ritual. Clyde was a dope fiend. He sat on a battered wooden bench and his lone figure cast a ten foot shadow, Clyde bowing at the foot of his shadow. Clyde, the high priest paying homage to his depraved god.

The stillness was broken by three cops. Two of them picked Clyde neatly off the bench, and the third held a young white kid in handcuffs. The cop looked down at his handcuffed prisoner who told him wordlessly with fear, that Clyde was definitely, most assuredly, the nigger who had sold him a bag of dope.

Flo turned off the radio when the phone rang and walked across the room snapping her fingers to the memory of some forgettable tune. She listened to Clyde's allotted phone call with a facial expression that can only be described as inscrutable. As she listened, she opened the drawer to the telephone stand and pulled out a pencil and pad. She wrote, "Arraignments-100 Centre St.—Tuesday—7:30 p.m.," then spoke with an abbreviated sigh, "Yeah Clyde—I got it." She hesitated, then hung up the receiver and started to walk back to the radio, when the sounds in the other room stopped her. She smirked. She walked back to the telephone stand and wrote underneath Clyde's message! "Bring the kid too—neither one of us will be seeing Clyde for a long time." She looked at the telephone, and anger washed her as she thought.

"No—not for a long time. We won't be seeing that stupid nigger. Selling dope to a WHITE kid! Why I gotta go downtown anyway? The judge just gonna look at Clyde's sheet, then take one look at that jive-ass little white boy and say 'Put that nigger in jail and throw the key down the drain.' "

She looked down and the reality of what she had written touched her. He was, in spite of everything, her man. Clyde. Helpless, loving, wonderful, strung-out Clyde. Her anger faded and Flo cried.

Flo and Jo Ann got off the "A" train at Franklin Street and following Clyde's instruction began to walk. Jo Ann thought of herself as a big time party girl, a professional finger-popper: she couldn't, wouldn't take anything seriously. She was good company.

Neither girl had seen this old section of town before, and the strangeness of the surroundings was a bad omen. Not that the girls were superstitious; it was just that they didn't like the vibrations they were getting. Looming up from the cobblestones were apartment buildings, grotesque monsters, almost hidden by mazes of iron framework called fire escapes. This time Jo Ann was silent as the girls made their way up the stairs of a dirty white building which was supposed to be the Palace of Justice.

Inside the corridors reeked of stale cigarette smoke, stale promises and hopes. The girls saw a list taped to a door; the list had Clyde's name on it, so they went inside. Flo walked to the front and got a seat so that she could see the "bullpen" where the prisoners were kept. No sign of Clyde. The bailiff read the first prisoner's name—something Rodriguez. A bewildered Spanish man came out. The bailiff read the charges faster than a tape recorder on rewind while Rodriguez stood tense, his hands clenched behind his back. Three lawyers surrounded Rodriguez talking at him, but he didn't understand a word; in the background the judge droned, $1,000 bail . . . $500 . . . can you raise $100 cash bail, Mr. Rodriguez?" No one spoke for Rodriguez and the bullpen swallowed him up faster than it had spit him into the arena.

A new judge turned arraignments into a comedy hour. It was his show and he knew it.

Two boys had been arrested for the second time by the same officer. . . . "Why don't you boys give someone else your business?"

A drug dealer couldn't pay a cash alternative. "Sales haven't been very profitable lately I guess."

He gives a bum in greasy dungarees and a torn sweatshirt $5,000 cash bail . . . "You must have $5,000, Mr. Jones." The legal aides were college kids getting a legal workout, and the District Attorney was running wild. He put on quite a show of his own but the judge was so involved in his own private Ed Sullivan hour that he did nothing about it. Flo wasn't smiling.

She saw Clyde in the bullpen. He was sweating and looked like he hadn't slept for several days. The bailiff called out two names and Clyde came out, followed by a teenage white kid named Jimmy and three cops. Jimmy's parents were already up front as Flo came up to the bench with Clyde Jr. Clyde had chosen to defend himself rather than be a pawn in the contract game between legal aide and district attorney. He was speaking to the judge and pointing behind him at Flo holding the kid—a sympathy play. The judge looked like he was going for it too. He gave Jimmy $100 cash bail which the parents moved to pay at once. He looked at Flo and Clyde Jr. and then spoke: "$10,000 cash bail . . ." The audience grew uneasy and someone murmured, "$10,000? What'd he do—try to kill Nixon or something?"

Clyde jumped down from the stage and embraced Flo and the baby before the guards jumped after him and forcefully separated the family. Clyde whispered, "Don't worry, sugar, I'll beat it—it's a hummer. . . ." As the guards carried him back to the bullpen he embraced the air with his eyes closed.

Jo Ann came up and pulled at Flo's coat, but Flo just stood at the foot of the arena, a detached figure underneath the huge painted letters, IN GOD WE TRUST. When they got outside it was raining and the warm drops mixed with Flo's icy tears.

Uptown in Harlem, a small overlord was in a very big rage. "Find that nigger Clyde," he shouted at three men who stood in his living room. All three men wore zipped-open windbreakers and cabbie hats; they were very much alike right down to the .45 caliber pistols stuck into their pants. They stood in the room with their heads down and their hands in their jacket pockets.

"What the fuck are you dudes doin'? You supposed to be the slickest contract men in Harlem? You ain't shit! Clyde's been out there sportin' on my money for three weeks and you can't find him. Listen, I got a business to take care of—I can't be lettin' niggers just take my cash. Clyde owed me money and then he stole a few pieces of dope behind that. If I let every nigger fuck with my cash like that, how long you think I'm gonna be in business? Clyde's walkin' around in Harlem spendin' my money right now and you jive-ass Royal Mounties can't find him—I thought you was always supposed to get your man . . ." He walked to the bookcase and pulled out an envelope from between two books, then he walked to the door, opened it, and gave the envelope to the first man in the hallway. "Y'all better show me some results—right now, I don't know why the fuck I'm payin' you. If you don't do something soon. I'm gonna have to go out and ice that nigger myself . . ."

Justice smiled down on a moonlit schoolyard. And three figures waited in the stillness.

WALTER MYERS

The Fare to Crown Point

Jimmy Little had been high nearly the entire night and was just coming down, digging the slow motion world around him, when he noticed the time. It was only seven o'clock. People still gray from sleep were tumbling mechanically from the anonymous rows of brownstones on Herkimer Street towards the subways. Old men wrestled cans of ashes curbward and stray cats muddled impatiently beneath the stoops. Jimmy knew that he would be straight until late afternoon but decided that he would try to score again anyway. He usually let each session take care of itself but he felt particularly good today and decided to take care of business early.

He remembered this chick he had seen over at Rudy's apartment building, that is to say, she lived across the hall from Rudy. Rudy had said that she worked part-time as a waitress from early in the morning until just after lunch.

Jimmy had wanted to know more about her but Rudy had been too busy at the time getting into his own thing, which was making out with the guys that came over to borrow money from him. Rudy used to snort a little and sometimes he'd pretend to be higher on pot than he really was. He worked as a tailor and always had money so when the guys who were strung out came around and hit on him, he always had a few dollars for them. In turn, he always had a little trade going for himself.

Jimmy had seen the girl when he was going to Rudy's pad to pass some time. She was a hard-looking white girl with red hair and a sprinkle of freckles around her nose. He had thought of hitting on her, putting out a line to see what she did with it, but Rudy wouldn't set it up. He thought that he would eventually hit on her anyway but right now he thought he'd make her apartment. Rudy said he never saw her doing anything so she must have some bread stashed somewhere.

Jimmy had just been milling it around in his mind, trying to decide whether or not he was going to do it when he found himself at Rudy's apartment building. The super was there, an old Puerto Rican cat who took his job too damn seriously. He kind of doubled as doorman, general fixer and anything else he could think of. When he was there, however, you weren't getting in unless you called up first on the intercom system and whoever it was that you called, rang the buzzer to let you in. Jimmy said he had come to see Rudy, rang Rudy's bell as the old guy watched suspiciously, then asked if he could go up and bang on the door as Rudy was a heavy sleeper. The super said no, he couldn't. Jimmy felt that he could have put up a front and got in anyway but decided not to bother.

It did make him mad that someone should keep him out, especially the officious acting super, and decided to make the hit anyway. He went around the corner and ducked into the service entrance and made his way past the washing-machine with the out-of-order sign on it and into the back yard. The yard was empty. There was a concrete walk which went around the house for about six feet and then gravel for twenty feet to the next building. Rudy lived on the second floor and from the way Jimmy figured it, the girl's apartment should be facing the back. He looked up at the two buildings and didn't see any signs of activity at any of the windows. He took a garbage can, turned it upside down and placed it beneath the extended ladder of the fire escape. He climbed on it and jumped to the bottom rung. He swung for a moment, looking about him for some sign that he had been seen and then swung his legs up and climbed to the first floor. The apartment there looked pretty nice as he peered through the window. He tried to lift the window and it slid up easily. He thought he might as well try that apartment but the smell of brewing coffee changed his mind instantly. He eased the window closed and went up to the second floor. Looking through the window he could see the door leading to the hallway. There was a piece of paper stuck in it and Jimmy felt that it must have been an advertsisement that someone had slipped between the door and the jamb, probably after having rung the bell. He tried the window and it was locked.

He could see that it was the ordinary twist kind of window lock and that it barely caught. He pushed on the top frame of the window and it gave just enough to disengage from the lock and he slid the window open, slipped in noiselessly and closed it behind him. Jimmy moved along the wall, listening for any sign of occupancy. He looked into the only other room of the apartment. It was empty. The bathroom door was open and it was also empty. He checked the front door to make sure that it was locked and looked out through the peephole to make sure that the hallway was clear. Then he took off his shoes and started to search the apartment.

Jimmy started with the living room, which was really a combination living room and dining area. He didn't think that he'd find anything there but checked it out anyway. The apartment looked shabbier than he thought it would, the furniture was the cheap kind with the dull brass legs that you got with a free nine by twelve rug or fifteen inch television. Jimmy had noticed, when he glanced into the bedroom, that she had piled a lot of her clothing on the bed. Probably laying them out to take to the cleaners later, he figured. Sloppy girls usually didn't have anything of value, he thought, not having the taste or need to buy expensive jewelry or clothing. He went through most of the drawers in the living room, not finding anything except a Statue of Liberty bank with a few coins in it that had "Welcome To New York" painted on the base. He even took some of the books from the shelves, holding them by the covers and shaking them in case she had hidden money in any of them.

The only thing that he got from the books were a few pictures of girls, standing and staring at the camera or next to a car with their hands on the front fenders. There was a picture of her parents, she had written Mom and Daddy on the back of the picture for some reason, and a little girl that Jimmy thought must have been the girl when she was younger. She had a radio with a cracked case which made it unpawnable. Next to it was a photo album, the kind with three compartments that stood up on a dresser with glass covering the pictures. One of the frames had a picture of her in it, complete with robe and diploma. Another frame had a larger picture of her parents and the third still held its original picture of Gregory Peck.

Jimmy went into the bedroom and started looking half-heartedly through the drawers. When he got to the third one he found a notebook. He opened it and there was money in it. He counted out nine one dollar bills. On the page was written, in a precise handwriting, Crown Point, one way, forty-two dollars. Under it was drawn a thermometer with forty-two places, nine of which had been filled in with red pencil. She was trying to save up the money to get back to Crown Point. The notebook was a diary, too. He sat on the edge of the bed and read the last page or two. It rambled on about wanting to go back home and not wanting to go back home and sounded, the way it was written, like a confession magazine. It mentioned Jeff, wondering what Mommy would think of him. Jimmy lost interest quickly and was about to put it all back again, minus the nine dollars, when there was a sudden noise behind him.

He caught his breath, turned sharply, and saw nothing. He thought that someone might have been under the bed or crouching on the other side of the bed. Jimmy stood quickly. The pile of clothing on the bed moved. He thought that it must be a cat under the coats but he looked under the bed just in case. He straightened up cautiously and pulled away one of the coats the girl had piled on the bed. It was heavier than he thought it should have been. When he had pulled it away he saw what had both made the noise and made the clothing move.

Wrapped in a soft blue blanket with satin edges was a baby. It was awake and sucking on one balled-up fist whenever it could get it to its mouth. A thin line of saliva went down its chin and disappeared into the folds of the blanket. The girl had wrapped cans of food and an iron in the coats and placed them on the bed on either side of the baby to keep him from rolling onto the floor. The first thought that Jimmy had was that the girl might have just run out to the store for a minute and was already on her way back. He closed the drawers, pushed the coat back over the baby, put his shoes back on and left by way of the window. When he got around to the front of the building the super gave him a look, meant to be knowing, and he winked back.

Jimmy had an electric reducing machine at home which he had been saving for an emergency. He decided to pawn it and then get some sleep. All that day the thought of finding the baby like that stayed in his mind like a movie he had seen long ago but couldn't quite remember.

When Jimmy woke up the next morning he checked his

finances and found out that he was in pretty good shape. He got his stuff together and went out into the street, having to come back twice, once for his sunglasses and once when he decided to wear his sneakers. It was raining lightly and he thought about getting a box of Frosted Flakes and going to a movie until it stopped, but for some reason the baby was still on his mind. Rudy had said that the girl worked every morning and he wondered if she left the baby there every day. He had himself together for the morning and he knew that he still had to make it for the afternoon. Still, he had time if he just made a quick check to see if the baby was really there again. He went into a drug store and called José and checked out his connection for later. José said that everything was straight and that he could pick up any time in the afternoon and asked him why he didn't come by with his guitar. Jimmy said that he had to get himself together. He had pawned his guitar a week earlier anyway but he didn't want to tell José. As soon as he had hung up he went over to the apartment. He had his mail bag, the one he had copped from a friend who worked as a Christmas temporary. He held it with his elbow and under his coat. The old Puerto Rican super wasn't there so he rang a whole row of bells and waited for someone to buzz back. As soon as someone did he went in and up to Rudy's apartment. He knocked on Rudy's door to see if he was in and there was no answer. Then he took his mail bag out from under his coat, slung it across his shoulder, and knocked on the girl's door. There was no answer and he knocked again. He also rang the bell but he knew that Rudy's bell didn't work and figured hers didn't either. There was no answer. He tried the door and it was locked. Jimmy put the mail bag back under his coat, went downstairs, then into the back yard and finally into the girl's apartment again through the fire escape window.

The baby was on the bed again. Jimmy pulled out the diary and looked in it but there didn't seem to be anything different. The girl probably hadn't even noticed the money missing.

The baby began to cry softly. The way that it whimpered, half crying, half making low, hoarse noises as if it had been crying a long time before, reminded Jimmy of his sister. Beverly used to cry like that when she was having asthma attacks. Then one morning he had been wakened by his mother early so that she could make the bed before the doctor came to see about Beverly. He remembered eating toast that his mother had made in the oven and Beverly, her thin brown arms looking like tree limbs, laying with her face to the wall. The doctor had given them some medication and told his mother to call if she became worse. Later the baby-sitter had called his mother at her job. Beverly had died.

Jimmy pushed the cans to one side and turned him over on his stomach. He still cried and Jimmy picked him up and bounced him a little on his knee until he stopped. There was a bracelet around the baby's wrist. It consisted of a couple of strands of thread with four blue beads with the baby's name printed in neat block letters. The baby was Jeff.

Jimmy was wearing sneakers and left them on though they were tracking a little dirt. He went into the other room, to the cooking area, and opened the halfsized refrigerator under the counter. He found a bottle of milk with a nipple on it, half full. He poured some water into a saucepan, not bothering to rinse out the remnants of spaghetti left in it, and put it on the stove. The baby began to cry again and Jeff took him back into the bedroom, sitting on the edge of the bed so they could both see themselves in the dresser mirror.

"Hey, Jeff, dig yourself!"

The baby stopped crying and started chewing on his fist again.

"What's wrong with your old lady, man? She out making her hustle and got you all strung out, huh? Bet you got you a five dollars a day milk Jones. If you could take care of business for yourself you'd make it, huh? Hey, dig us in the mirror. That's me on the right, the black cat. Bet I'm the first black cat you ever dug, huh? You see me, man? Hey, Jeff!"

Jimmy heard the water come to a boil and went and got the bottle. He sprinkled a few drops on his wrist, watching them run along the contrasting darkness of his own skin, and realized that he didn't know why people sprinkled milk on their wrists. He had seen women do it, but didn't know if the milk should be cool, hot or what.

"If this shit is too hot, my man, you just gonna have to let me know."

Jeff took the bottle hungrily, making loud sucking noises which seemed to fill the room. Jimmy let him finish the bottle and then he put the baby back down on the bed, watched it throw up a little, decided that it was all right and went back to reading the diary. It was mostly uninteresting. Jimmy wondered what made her put in such trivial shit. She had written her name in the book on the front page. Jimmy wondered what kind of person would put her own name on the front page of a diary. Her name was Kathy Moffett and she had come to New York from Crown Point, Indiana. It went on about how she had been looking for a job and finally found one and then how lonely she was. It was funny to see someone write it down, that they were lonely. It was the kind of thing that you knew about and sometimes felt but there was a sadness to it when it was written in a book. I am so lonely, she had written, I am so lonely. She had only come to New York for the summer before she entered school and she had met some man at a party who had taken her home and slept with her. There was a lot of stuff about how ashamed she was at what she had done. She kept talking so much about what she had done that Jimmy read the first part again, thinking that he must have missed something but found that the only thing she had done was to get laid.

She had become pregnant with Jeff and the man told her that he was married and that he didn't love her anyway and she started putting in things about killing herself. She also said that things weren't any different in New York than they were in Crown Point. Jimmy skipped a few pages until he got to the part about her naming the baby after her father. Her parents didn't know about Jeff yet and she was trying to get enough money together to get a ticket back home to Crown Point. She was on welfare now. Jimmy figured she was sneaking in a few hours of work at the restaurant for the extra money.

There was some noise outside the apartment and Jimmy

heard Rudy's voice. He crossed over to the peephole and saw Rudy going into his apartment with a young boy. Jimmy smiled at the idea of Rudy picking up some trade in the middle of the day. He checked the time and saw that it was almost lunchtime and figured that he had maybe an hour or so before the girl came back. The morning had gone faster than he thought. He was beginning to feel badly anyway. At first he thought it was the rain but then he saw through the yellowed chiffon curtains that the sun had brightened the clouds. Jimmy figured he'd fix himself up with the stuff he had and then go to the park for his high before he looked around for another score.

He heated his stuff in the kitchen. He had noticed that there was some alcohol on the dresser and he wiped the end of his needle off with it although he had never really been concerned with infection before. He dropped his pants, flexed the long muscles in his thigh until he found his line and popped. He was taking down his needle when he noticed that the baby was looking in his direction. He swung his hand, the slap turning the baby's face. For a moment the baby was silent, trying to catch his breath. Then he started crying as loudly as he could. Jimmy picked him up and held him against his chest.

"Hey, dig, my man, I'm sorry. I blew. You can't dig my changes, I know that. Yeah, I'm sorry. You got your own changes to go through." Jimmy rocked and patted the baby until he stopped crying and stuck an unsure hand into Jimmy's face. Jimmy put him down gently in the middle of the bed, reassembling his little fortress of coats and cans.

"Can't stand for nobody to see me on my string, Jeff."

Jeff was looking at his fingers, opening them and closing them.

Jimmy pulled his pants up quickly, put his equipment away, got his mail bag from the dresser and went out the window, coming back once to make sure that he hadn't left the gas on.

The first thing he did when he hit the street was to buy a large mission soda and then he went into the park to get into his high. He sat on the bench, down from some checker players, and flowed into it, all the while thinking about the baby. He wondered what he could buy for it and whether or not its mother gave a damn for the little fellow. Maybe, he thought, he would buy it something nice, something that made a noise so he wouldn't feel so alone during the day.

The wind awakened him and he found himself pulling his jacket together at the collar. He discovered that he had peed on himself. Every time he went into a real bad high, coming off an argument with his mother or while depressed, he always peed on himself. It made him real mad and he always came down hard, never easing out of it like when he was together with himself. It was almost dark. He had to score and make it over to José's place for the night session. He went through his pockets and found a dollar and thirty-seven cents. After cleaning himself up in the park rest room he started cross town, stopping at a delicatessen for some cup cakes and another soda.

The only way he was going to get some money in a hurry, he knew, was to cop from somebody on the way over to

José's house. He thought about asking José to turn him on to a nod but he knew that he wouldn't. He even thought of going over to Rudy's but he didn't feel like going through Rudy's changes.

It was a woman, an old woman, that he saw paying for some rutabagas at an outdoor market with a ten dollar bill. Jimmy followed her down the street, trying not to think of taking the money from her or that she looked, with her black ex-Sunday coat on, so much like his own mother, or that he might have to hurt her. He wished that he had eaten something solid. She turned into a doorway on Gates Avenue and Jimmy followed, closing the distance between them. He caught her on a turn as she went up the stairs, stepping aside in deference to the youthful footballs behind her. He grabbed her ankles and jerked them from under her. Her knees hit the stairs hard, one barely catching the edge of the step, pulling the tin away. Jimmy was vaguely aware of the sounds she made, the clumping and the small cry of pain as she half slid down the steps. He grabbed her pocketbook, having to snatch it from the still tight grip, and ran out of the hall. The street was nearly deserted except for a group of girls turning double dutch at the corner. The bus to Civic Center was passing and he got on. The bus driver looked at the pocketbook and at Jimmy and Jimmy shoved it under his coat. He got off at the next dark street and took the money out of the pocketbook and putting the pocketbook itself into a mailbox. The money was more than he had imagined that it would be, nearly eighty dollars. He hailed a cab to José's place.

Jimmy bought his stuff from José. He also copped for the next day. José and his old lady, Margie, wanted to shoot up with him. Jimmy said no, knowing that they would be mostly shooting up on his money. Besides, he didn't have to shoot up right then and wasn't in the mood to party. It would have been down to shoot up with Margie though, he thought, she was a fine chick and always started reciting poetry and going through some kind of freak scene when she got high.

The next day he went to the five and ten and bought a small blue duck for Jeff. He had started to get him a rubber Popeye, one like he used to have with a metal thing in the bottom that squeaked when you squeezed it, but he figured that Jeff probably couldn't squeeze it hard enough anyway.

It was a warm day. In a week or two the weather would break and things would pick up. There were two little boys in Rudy's yard sneaking a smoke and Jimmy took the cigarettes from them and made them leave the yard. When they had gone he pulled the can over to the fire escape, this time scraping his knee badly as he swung himself up the ladder. He tried to remember if the girl had any Bandaids in the medicine cabinet. He opened the window, slipped into the apartment and out of his shoes. He went immediately into the bedroom to say hello to Jeff and found the girl sitting on the bed with the baby.

"Don't scream or I'll kill you!" Jimmy was surprised by the gruff sound of his voice.

"I—I won't." She was shaking her head no. She was less attractive than her pictures, seeming more unhealthy than ugly. The blue of her eyes, alive and sparkling in Jeff, was faded and without expression in his mother.

"How come you're home today?" Jimmy asked.

She didn't answer but started to cry. Her mouth moved once or twice as if she might speak but nothing came out. She gestured to the open drawer where her diary and money had been. Finding himself in control of the situation, Jimmy became aware again of his aching knee. He thought of things to say to her, about leaving the baby, about the diary, and even of his aching knee. She was holding Jeff in front of her, clinging to the child, her shoulders rising with her silent sobbing. Jeff began to laugh at the movement against his stomach. Jimmy tossed the toy to the foot of the bed.

In the living room he took out forty-two dollars, the fare to Crown Point, and laid it on the dresser in front of her picture album. He left this time by the front door. He had almost reached the stairs when he stopped. Blood had seeped through his pants leg at the knee and the fabric was beginning to stick to him. If the girl hadn't been there he would have fixed it up in the apartment.

Jimmy went back to the apartment, tried the door and it opened. He glanced into the bedroom and she had turned on her side, half curling her body around Jeff, facing away from the door. Jimmy took the money from the table and put it in his pocket.

After taking half of the money home and putting it behind a drawer he got the crosstown bus to José's house to shoot up with José and Margie. Jeff and his mother, he thought, would have to score for themselves.

LINDSAY PATTERSON

Miss Nora

Miss Nora Green's small clapboard house always smelled of freshness inside, and this Sunday a stray breeze, finding it could not deodorize any of the house's three gleaming rooms, moved swiftly out into the day.

Nora sat in her front room with the comic section of the *Lafayette Times*, reading and rereading slowly and thoughtfully each word. To be sure first that she knew each word's meaning, and then to be sure that she grasped the humor of them all. And when finally deciding she had missed nothing, she rested the paper on her lap, threw back her head and rolled in laughter, her fat body shaking and her small, brown eyes darting and flashing with the luminosity of lightning bugs in her dark oval face. After a few minutes, she folded the paper carefully, tucked it away in a remote corner of the tiny parlor, then went out on her porch, saddled herself in a high-back chair, and waited for the Sunday strollers to greet her.

Everybody knew Nora. People called her the "pleasantest" woman alive. Although Nora was forty-five years old and had never been married, no one ever thought of her as being an old maid or lonely except Nora herself. Whenever it did come up that Nora wasn't married, everyone agreed that she found so much happiness within herself she needed no one.

"No man can give Nora the happiness she got," said Elsa Brown to her pinochle club one night. "If I could be as happy as she is without any attachment, I'd throw my nigger out and just live from day to day. Every time I see Nora lately she gets fatter and happier. It's a sin to be so happy."

No one suspected Nora's happiness lay at that very moment within her body developing. Nora had always wanted children of her own, and now that a child would be born to her she felt the unrestained excitement of a mother-to-be.

She was especially happy this Sunday because she could feel the child forming and moving around within her. She wished that it were already born, and that she was coddling and kissing it and holding it to her breast. "My very own child. Nobody's but mine," she meditated.

Her employers had three girls and when they were very young she mothered them, but now they were nearing adulthood and refused to recognize her as any more than a servant. She loved them in spite of their indifference for her motherly concern, and never ceased performing functions their own mother found distasteful. She was often severely rebuked for overstepping her boundary, but she dismissed their objections with a short, happy laugh, while feeling very much the pain inside.

The Sunday parade of walkers started. Some lingered and chatted briefly about the day and the weather reports for the days in store. Others commented upon the neat front yard with special admiration for her flowers and foliage.

"Miss Nora," called one young girl, "how do you get your stuff to grow in this red clay? Lawd, you sure knows your business. I plant manure and nothing comes up. And I says to myself, 'Miss Nora with her magic should come over and touch these things and I bet they'd grow!'"

Nora laughed, and the girl joined in, too. Each stroller always ended with a comment on how well Nora looked.

"Miss Nora, you look plumb pretty. The fatter you get, the prettier you look. You look like you regressed in age. Now take me. I'm about your age and I shows it. Plumb pretty you are."

Nora would again shake in laughter, then disclaim to her admirers that she looked as good, and they promptly assured her that in their eyes she did, and this would call for more laughter.

As the summer light grew dim, the strollers were fewer, and when only thistles of stars made patterns in the night, Nora moved slowly inside her house while listening attentively for footsteps on the street. Inside the house, she switched on the single light that strung down from the ceiling. She blinked and then squinted her eyes at the strong light and thought wisely to herself that she must get a smaller bulb before the baby came because she did not want to damage its eyes. She sat down on the couch, taking care that the three doilies on the back of it would not be mussed.

Nora did not have many visitors in her house, and when she did expect any she made elaborate preparations for their comfort: she would scrub and polish until the very grain of her floors and fabrics were visible. But there was one visitor she made little preparation for. He came every Sunday night at eleven o'clock.

It was nowhere near eleven now, and Nora was content to sit and think about the formation inside her. She prayed nightly that it would be a boy. They don't cry and carry on like little girls, was one of her reasons. And this house needs a man around it, she had said many times to herself. She thought, too, about all the infant ware she had admired in the town's department store. She had touched and fingered the colthes every day for the last two weeks, and thought it foolish to constantly look and not buy. Daily, she had commanded herself not to go back into the store until after the baby was born, but, always, at some point during the day, something seemed to have led her to the store, then snatched her inside without her consent.

She dozed, but the chiming of the clock for ten made her wide-awake and caused her to shift her thought from within to the open window. For the first time that night, she realized it was cooler inside the small square room than it had been all summer. She got up from the couch and walked to the window, pulling the yellow paper shade down until it shut out the night. Next, she went to the screen door and made sure it was unhooked. As she neared the center of the room on her way back to the couch, she reached up and turned off the light, and then in the darkness found the couch and sat down gingerly, fearful again that she might mess up her doilies.

She waited stoically in the darkness, for she knew that before the clock hit the eleventh hour, he would be walking through the door. She sang a lullaby softly to herself as she waited.

It was not long before footsteps thumped on the porch and stopped. The screen door creaked open and closed without a sound. There, outlined against the door was the lean figure of a man proportioned justly from his head to his hips, only to be supported, cruelly, by one elephantine leg and one slightly shriveled.

"Nora, Nora. Where are you?" the man called.

"Here on the couch. I'm on the couch."

"Need some goddamn light in this place," the man complained, and following the sound of her voice, inquired, "Nothing in my way?"

"No, there ain't ever anything in the way."

He took careful steps across the room and bumped against the couch.

"You here?" said Nora, matter-of-factly.

He laughed and plopped down almost on top of her, and she slid over just in time, missing the force of his body as he sank awkwardly into the soft cushions. The man reached out in the darkness to feel Nora, and her whole body pulsated as he ran his hands first across her breast and then down to her thighs. His hands lingered on her stomach.

"Nora," the man said "you've been putting on weight lately and I like it."

The man pulled Nora to him. He leaned over her in the darkness and with his damp tongue out, grappled for her mouth. She jerked away.

"What's the matter, Nora?"

"I just don't feel much like it tonight," she mumbled. She could feel the forming baby move around.

"No one else has had you, have they?" he asked sharply.

"No. Ain't nobody but you."

Nora could no longer control her excitement, and told the man about the baby. His face lit up with pride. He relaxed his clutch on her body and simply squeezed her hand.

"It'll be a boy," she said. "I know it will."

Nora, her eyes closed, felt so happy that she wanted to cry. But cry she never did, neither for joy nor for sadness. Her position in life had made her immune to an emotion so unstable.

Later, Nora felt the man struggling to get up, and when she reached out in the darkness to touch him, she only felt the dampness on the couch.

"What's wrong, honey?" she asked, puzzled.

The man's thumping gait had stopped before the screen door and she saw through misty eyes her boy, twenty years hence, silhouetted there; his shoulders as broad as the man's, his height the same, and his legs, unlike the man's, straight and firm. She could imagine no deformity in her boy as she saw in the man. When she knew about the baby, she had started to make plans for its education—to send it away to school and "have him talking like he was somebody." She had five-hundred-and-twenty-three dollars and eighteen cents in the bank and she figured that, coupled with another twenty years of work, would do. "Yes," Nora reflected, "he is going to *be* really something."

The man turned from the door and spoke crisply to Nora.

"Here's fifty dollars," he said, taking the money out of his wallet and laying it on a table beside the door and the summer breeze in its last effort of the night flipped the money up and sent it whirling through the room, till it landed silently on the darkened floor.

Nora slowly realized that she should not have confided in the man. Revulsion hammered in her breast. The dampness she sat in no longer warmed her, and she tried to repudiate it, perceiving that it was out to consume her.

"I don't want none of your money," she managed to shout.

"God will spite it," the man said.

"Ain't none of His business," cried Nora.

A strange satisfaction had engrossed the man, yet he continued to speak with vengeance. "He will spite it," he said again, and miraculously blended into the darkness.

Nora remained sitting in her parlor for the remainder of the night, her face pursed in a scowl for perhaps the first time in her life.

The following Sunday, Nora sat in her front room with the comic section of the *Lafayette Times*, reading and re-reading slowly and thoughtfully each word. To be sure first that she knew each word's meaning, and then to be sure that she grasped the humor of them all. And when finally deciding she had missed nothing, she rested the paper on her lap, threw back her head and rolled in laughter, her fat body shaking and her small, brown eyes darting and flashing with the luminosity of lightning bugs in her dark oval face. After a few minutes, she folded the paper carefully, tucked it away in a remote corner of the tiny parlor, then went out on her porch, saddled herself in a high-back chair, and waited for the Sunday strollers to greet her.

"Miss Nora," called one young girl, "the fatter you get, the prettier you look."

Nora shook in laughter, then disclaimed that she looked as good, and the girl promptly assured her that in her eyes she did.

ERIC PRIESTLEY

The Seed of a Slum's Eternity

On the ground. That's where the brother was when I saw him. On his back. Yeah. Me and my patna had just turned the corner and there was the brother on his back with his hands up and they're both shakin'. At first I thought he had the palsy or something before I dug what that brother who was standing over him was holdin'. This cat had a hammer in his hand, and he had it drawn back threatening to bust this brother's brains out. There were two cats doing their best to hold him off the dude, but he got a chance to swing the hammer anyway, and as the dude on the ground squirmed to his side, his face looked like a rat's that done stole a piece of cheese before the trap snapped. Then I hear the hammer hit the ground, saw bright red sparks shoot off the asphalt and set the cold black night on fire. I rubbed my head in my hands and said "Lord have mercy."

Then they got to arguing, but the brother still held the

hammer in his hand. They tried to get it away from him but he wouldn't let it go. I told my patna, "Man get your car out the street and go on and park. These niggas done gone crazy again." We sat there and watched them till they went away. Niggas went away rappin. Seem like their shadows melted into the black night they come out of:

"Naw nigga don' nobody want to hear that. Naw . . . naw."

"Look here brother! . . ."

"Dig you a fool. Now won't you listen?"

"Naw nigga I don't want to hear that shit . . . naw . . . naw." Then dead silence, except for the jogging and the jerking and the screeching of the freight train at the end of the block. Yeah. A cold black night without no moon. No light. Nothin' but the bright orange glow of them red flames coming out the stack of that metal facory 'cross the railroad tracks.

Here we go! This is how the seed grow baby. HummmmmmmmmmmmmmmmmmmHere we gooooooo . . . HUmmmmmmmmmmmmmmm Hum a little. Here we gooooooooooo. Rock a Li'l. HummmmmmmmmmmmHum a Li'l. Here we gooooooooooooooo. Rock a Li'l. Hummmmmmmmmmmmm Hum a li'l. I say can everybody feel it? Yeah.

I had a friend, but he died. I wanted to write. Couldn't. Cried. Wanted to sing, but didn't have no voice. Wanted to whistle through the dank gray dawn dipped in rain. Yeah! Whistle something sad . . . whistle love . . . whistle pain. Go away, but none of that happened. Didn't nothin' go right.

Felt blamed, maimed. Twisted in a thorny briar of thought and fault . . . fault unfounded. And I was the scapegoat. . . . Dubbed the doer of evil, that was me the prize of tragedy. Couldn't tame the roar of angry voices that cried out with fist cracking upside my head after funerals. And around me a bunch of dead fools who clammed up when they really tried to love anybody, cause they had been drinking "calm" and forgot the rest of their lines.

Sho' was cold when Tenatche come over the pad that evenin' with her head all bandaged up. Both her eyes was blacked and swollen. She didn't say nothin' . . . had tears in her eyes. Told me to come there and let her show me something. I told her alright and took her in the room. She pulled her dress up . . . didn't have no panties on. I didn't know what the hell was happenin', till I looked. I'd neva seen nothin' like that in my life. Big round purple blue circles all over the side of her ass . . . welped up bad by the hip bone. Bruised so bad the spots were blotches. Heavy and thick with blood beneath the skin. Skin so red and flushed it looked like it was gonna pop! I say:

"Girl, what in the hell happened to you? Put your dress down." She did. Kept on crying and say:

"My mama beat me with a hammer."

I say: "With a what?"

She say: "With a hammer. I been in the hospital. My skull is fractured. She knocked me out. She tried to kill me."

I say: "What did she do that for?"

She say: "'Cause I bought a dress."

I shook my head and say, "Ain't this a mess." And she left

139

crying. I saw her mama couple of weeks later. She said Tenatche was lying, and ain't that the way the seed grow, baby? But Tenatche sho' came by, and she sho' had the marks of a hammer. And there ain't no denying that she sho' left crying. Yeah. But when I saw her mama, she said Tenatche was lying. Marks of a hammer. Tenatche left crying. Shit somebody lying, but the seed grows true, though the plant ain't bloomed and the man ain't grown.

Patnas dying. Everybody droppin' them pills. Brothers and sisters droppin' dead all around you. Ain't none of this no good. Finding dead bodies. Testifying at trials. People threatening to kill you. Ain't things bad enough? Kids outside throwing bottles. Hear them breaking in the alley? Alleys filled to overflowing with broken glass and beer cans, and dry brown blood splotches that got spilled over razor fast dice.

"If you can't gamble you ought to stay off the corner punk."

The ice man is a shrewd looking dude in a Cadillac. Wears fancy French cuff-links with them big collar shirts. The idol of all the young hipsters. Got a bitch talk faster than him, and it's understood that she carry a gun. And that thing between her legs is a moneymaker. Yeah! Talkin' 'bout a gold mine. Five dollars a ton for fifteen minutes. and the whore shoot more smack than the law allow. Keep her man hollering 'bout her habit, but like she say: "I got to have it baby, I just got to have it."

Walkin' and talkin' on my way to the store in the morning. There was an old cat standing across the street. Had on a pair of baggy striped pants. Fly was open. Drunk as he could be. An old brown hat crumpled on his head wrinkled and worn from the sun and lack of care. The band soaked with sweat. Showing the toil of days working for a short dog of wine. I dug him close, just as I had dug Shorty a million times coming across the tracks on 103rd so 'jacked' up he couldn't see.

As I walked to the black store on the corner, which ain't nothin' but a hole in the wall, but everybody went there 'cause if you didn't the nosey ass neighbors got to rappin 'bout:

"That nigga ain't got no race pride."

"That's why niggas ain't got nothing. You see he'll go to the Jew around the corner though, don't you?"

"We don't patronize our color."

All this was going on in my head as I stepped over the sewer and crossed to the corner.

I say, "Alright . . . alright. What's goin' on, brother?"

He say, "Ain't nothin' goin' on."

I say, "Naw. You got the best 'hand.' If I had yours I'd turn mine in backwards."

He spoke loud as he could, "Yeah? Well you sho' wouldn't have nothin', 'cause my hand is wrote in the 'shitter.' "

Then he spit through his teeth, shaped his old beat-up hat to the side and leaned hard on his cane. I dug his eyes and they were cold and blood-red and he wasn't bullshittin' a pound. I kept on steppin' and as I went to walk off the curb it hit me and I tripped thinking, "Yeah, patna. I don't know old man. Maybe mine is wrote in there too."

You know what they say about me? They say, "That nigga

smart. He go to school. He can write, but he can't spell. You
know he don't go to church. He gonna' burn in hell."

My old man used to work on the railroad. Caught menin-
gitis and near 'bout died. Got hit by a taxi cab and dragged
nine blocks. Been shot in the leg with a forty-five. Stabbed
in the thigh by a whore named Georgia. Ain't got a dime to
show for the job, and nothin' but scars and misery for the
rest. He had another little "slave" "round the corner," or
"'cross the tracks," or "pushin' a broom in the evening." Lost
all that. Too old. Early retirement. Nothin' go right down
here.

I ride the bus. It ain't so bad. You get to pick your nose in
private. Thump the *buggas* on the floor and look at the bums
on 4th and 5th and Main. Like the one I saw this morning
lying in the doorway across the street from the mission. An
empty bottle of port wine by his head. Gray head. What
wasn't gray had turned white. I mean he was right. I'm not
jivin'. He was right in the right spot, 'cause I noticed in the
brown doorway above where he slept was printed just as
plain as you wish "FUCK THE U.S.A." I'm telling you the
shit is real. If you don't believe me, go down there on 4th
street across from the mission and see for yourself. Right
there on Main. I don't know his name, 'cause he was just a
bum. Yeah, just another bum. On 4th and Main. Lying half
in the sun. Full of that wine. In the right spot all alone.
Another bum in L.A. in the right spot at the right time, lying
in a doorway, full of that wine beneath the words "FUCK
. . . THE . . . U.S.A." I started to laugh, but it wasn't funny,

'cause that hard ass cement was his bed. That wine was his weakness. Kismet? He sho' picked a cold blooded spot.

There are other bums. Ride down a little further to Olvera Street and dig the Leprechaun bum. Now he's the real trip. He got a little metal shopping cart full of rags and he so black with dirt you don't know if it's color. One day I dug him up close when he was scratching his nasty ass beard. Talking 'bout a beard. A beard with lice. Lice that bite, 'cause he sure was scratching 'em. Olvera Street. Yeah you know where that is. During the "Boxer Rebellion" it was called "nigger alley." On Alameda and Macy. You know down there by the P.O., that's where the cotton sack was taken out of the nigga's hand, and the mail sack put in. I do not talk revolution. Revolution talks for itself.

Or we can go up on the end. Yeah. THE END. You know where that is. That's where the niggas sell smack. Also where a lot of brothers talk Voodoo, piss in the alley, on the sidewalk, wherever they please, and don't give a fuck.

I didn't even know there had been a cutting, until Meatball came by my pad and showed me the twenty-eight stitches in his mug. He was "jacked" up . . . lip all hanging. And for what? It sho' was stupid. Meatball got his throat cut over two dollars and a radio, that was probably stolen anyway. From then on he was leary 'bout letting people get close to him but twenty-eight stitches with a straight razor hadn't kept the dude from giggin' with the rhythms of his soul. He kept right on going through a bunch of fast changes and the street life. The get high. The corner. The same bitches giving up pussy, but no money. Brothers were sayin', "Shit, a good cutting will change anybody's life. Life or death you bound to change." But Meatball was just another tangent gettin' sliced away. Wasn't no way out of eternity. Not for Meatball. Nothin'. That was all, 'cause he came from infinite nothin'. Nothin' of air . . . nothin' of earth. Nothin' of fire . . . nothin' of water. Nobody mattered down here, 'cause there was nothin' in the filth. Nothin' in the vomit-filled alleys, of 'wolf ticket' selling moles who didn't spare talking 'bout a chump's mama. Got used and gammed on. Tricked and played on, just like the rest of the dudes walking around that didn't know what was happening.

Wandering through an empty house. Everyone was gone. The candles drew spectral figures on the walls. Thick walls. Smoke-stained walls. Alone. Thinking was it all worth telling. Worth the romance. Worth the wasted feelings in putting it down. It's hard to prowl like a hungry night cat stalking images and putting words to paper. Running away. Finding that no sense was made of lunacy. No peace found in silence. Almost wishing that I hadn't started to think about the shit.

Holding your "mug" can become a jive habit. For Meatball and a lot of other brothers, the slum was like being under the ground. Like being beneath the surface of the earth living like insects and rats in the crowded caverns of a sewer. I don't like a bunch of frontin' fat mouthing suckas. And a lot of brothers believed that it had been God's will that the brother got cut, but I thought that was a lot of bullshit. Then, too, the word was that the other cat was defending himself against Meatball, 'cause he had a knife and was trying to stab the cat when they were fighting in the kitchen.

Damn near stabbed him too. When he swung the dude moved and the knife broke off against the ice box. You see there is no compassion in the hole. No compassion in me or Meatball or anybody.

'Bout two days later my house burned down and all of . . . Meatball's stuff was in there. . . . Brothers were talkin' 'bout somebody had sabotaged the place.

"Man, this sho' is cold. I had 'bout three hundred and fifty dollars worth of rags in that pad," says Meatball. I didn't think that Meatball ever had that much money, let alone that much clothes, but that wasn't the point. My house had been burned down and all this nigga's rags with it and he was madder than a mothafucka. So I thought: "The whiteman ain't gonna' have to destroy Black people. We're doing it ourselves."

Now Serphronia was did. And this means just what it says. The sister was good, but she got did by the town. Did by the slum. The chump rappin' 'bout *the way of all flesh* blew the understatement of the century. Serphronia went too cold. Straight down the middle of the Sunset Strip. Butt naked. With a flower painted on her chest. "In between her breast" is what I heard. Yeah and there she went steppin'. Some brothers said, "At least the sista styled." Styled she did till the police busted her. Took her to Camarillo. The drums I got said Serphronia was trippin' off "acid." Yeah. Deep, deep trip. Tripped by the people and then she said, "Fuck the world."

Two weeks before, Leopold's sister shot herself in the head. Shot herself dead. It sho' is cold down here. Brothers don't even want to go to funerals lately. They been so many.

Then I was walking to the slave one day. A bright clear day. There were two carpenters nailing on the top of a roof, and as I passed below on the pavement I had to shade my eyes from the sun. One of them carpenters got to foaming at the mouth and spittin' nails like he'd gone stone crazy, then he took his hammer and threw it hard as he could at the sun. And he kept on cussin', and shakin' his fist. His patna tried to calm him and help him off the ladder to the ground, but he wouldn't move, he just kept on cussin' and shakin' his fist. I just shook my head and kept on walking. Pass the kids with the B.B. guns trying to bring a hawk down off a telephone wire. The people went running and gathered at the bottom of the house crying: "Look at him. Look at him. He done gone crazy and throwed his hammer at the sun." I went in the liquor store. A pusher bobbin' on the corner pulled my coat: "Betta come on and get some of this dynamite, baby." Flashing the many colored balloons in his palm.

I say, "Naw, homeboy, I don't want no smack."
I kept steppin'. Went in the store and copped a short dog of bitter lemon. I went outside and dug over in the corner. As usual, big as life, 'bout ten brothers was squatted down. Yellin' seven come eleven. Flashing money and steady rappin':

"Ah man. Put the damn money back down. You faded me the last time. Why you gonna be so cold baby."

"Fuck you punk. This ain't no charity game. Bet on your own dice, suckah."

"Great God in the mornin'. Looka here I done hit again."

"Be sweet to me dice, hot honies, 'cause daddy needs the money."

"Looka here, I'm on fire. Hit again and I'll break this mothafucka."

"Bet, nigga . . ."

"Nigga, I done bet. You the one ain't got no money down."

"Just bet, nigga. Bet. The money is good."

Flashing bills crumpled in sweaty hands. Black jackets, knives and guns, and as I walked away I could still hear: "Bet, nigga. Bet."

I hit my bottle of wine on the bottom before I spun the cap and it fell off as I began to walk down the alley. Thinking of eternity. Eternity in an alley. Sick of things the way they were. Didn't even go to work, 'cause I knew I wasn't gonna make no money down there. I damn sho' wasn't gonna make no money in that alley, but that's the way it is in the slum. Wasn't nothin' gonna change. Not that I could see, and I took a drink of wine and got to singing and thinking about eternity:

I'm a straight talking railroad man. And I'm the head of the Klu/Klux/Klan. I say I'm a hard working railroad man. And I'm the head of the Klu/Klux/Klan . . .

And I mean I'm walkin' and rockin'. Rockin' and walkin'. Swaying with the soft breeze that blew pass my ears and singing:

I'm a straight razor carrying railroad man. And I'm the head of the Klu/Klux/Klan.

A Right Proper Burial

Brown looked like a giant as he sat by the lake not thinking of anything except, "Christ, you are a good man in spite of this." On the shore, he sat mumbling words of hatred, evil words that played on his mind and would not let him sleep.

"It's autumn," he said. "Yeah, but who gives a damn, 'cept witches and jack-o-lanterns? I'm just an old spade cat," he mumbled. "Ain't nobody gonna do nothing for me, so I got to help myself." The water rippled slightly, fish lapped at the surface, ripples spread like disease.

Brown stood up, mumbled, laughed, hawked and spit. Ripples rippled. He looked across the lake, gauging with one eye the distance to the other side. It would be a long way across. He tried to picture it. How he would do it. Could he make it? He smiled. He sure had put one over on the folks in town, on that high-faluting Reverend and all the others.

"Hypocrites," Brown thought, "standing there with their eyes closed."

He laughed, then sat on the leaves that had fallen sometime before this time they call autumn. His belly convulsed. Out of the bag in his back pocket, he lifted a bottle and took a drink. Soft fluid dribbled down his chin, down his soft, brown skin. "These are bad times," he thought. He re-capped the bottle, and rested it beside him.

"Gonna just fold my hands," he said. "Ain't gonna worry 'bout nothing. Don't nobody care no how." And he did just that—folded his hands over his belly, closed his eyes, 'cause wasn't nothing to worry about anyhow. There wasn't nobody who was gonna steal that little coffin, with pretty little Bellinda inside.

More leaves fell on the fallen ones, and on Brown, and on the coffin a short distance away. Brown was set. Wasn't nobody gonna take that coffin, wasn't nobody gonna hurt Bellinda anymore, wasn't nobody gonna touch nothing 'cept him, and he knew that. He wept when he remembered.

Brown uncapped the bottle again, and took another drink. Silly to think a tormented man could sleep. He drank the bottle empty, then swung it with his arm, letting it fly into the water. Ripples rippled. "Ohhhhhhh, I'm just an old spade cat," Brown sang. His head fell heavy against the ground, and he rolled in the damp leaves, and cursed, and beat his belly, and cried.

"Lawd kill me!" he screamed, then he apologized for his sacrilege, and mumbled. He thought he heard footsteps. All of a sudden he rolled over, and jumped to his feet. Brown darted for the coffin, madly scooping up leaves and throwing them over the brown wood box. Then he ran for the big tree he'd spotted in that split second between fear and discovery.

He peered from behind the tree, peered as much as he dared. His breathing was heavy. Small clouds of smoke rounded from his mouth to his nostrils, and his hands pulled anxiously at the bark.

"Ain't nobody here," said the tall, dark man in the leather jacket. "Brother Brown must've got away." This man had a powerful, distinctive voice. He kicked at the damp leaves. Idly. He was quickly joined by two other men.

They talked, looking across the wide-stretching lake, looking at the sky's reflection in the water—blue on blue, leaning against itself. Brown could hear them clearly. He recognized each voice. They had tracked him from the church. His heart felt like it was sinking inside him, washed inward by his warm body's blood.

"Ol, Brown never *was* too right in the head," the man in the leather jacket said. "Poor ol' devil, taking a coffin like that. Well, come on." His companions approached. "Let's go get Ben Davis and his dogs and bring 'em down here." They started off, but one man held back.

"Maybe I'd better wait here, case Brown shows up. I can pose myself 'hind one of them trees."

"And what happens if Brown comes up behind you, while you're busy looking off in the wrong direction?" asked the man in the jacket. "Brown culd just about crush a man with his weight. Oh, no. We'd best stick together." The other man did not argue. He followed sulkily behind his friends, and all three walked off in the direction of the ridge from which they had come.

Seeing them leave, Brown slowly slid around from behind the tree. Sweat streamed from his face. He'd held himself so tense, so rigid, his neck ached. "Brown done gone, boys," he mumbled. "Brown done gone, boys." He crouched down, and hurried towards the coffin.

He fell to his knees and swept the leaves away. His breathing turned to spurts of gasping and panting. "Don't you worry none, honey," he said. "Ol' Brown is here, and he gonna see that you gets home safely. Yes he is." He put all his tremendous weight behind the coffin, and pushed it toward the water. Ripples heaved away and the coffin floated off, Brown running in behind it.

He pushed the water with one hand. His feet kicked with terrific force. Water swirled and lapped against them. There was very little current. After a while, the continuous movement of his great arm caused his chest muscles to pain sharply. The cold water numbed his body. He thought about draping himself on top of the coffin, but was afraid of sinking it. "What I gonna do, Lawd?" He tried to think. His mind was as numb as his body.

Suddenly, Brown lifted his head. He could hear the baying of dogs and he could see several men running along the shore. He heard the low, heavy voices of men shouting to him. His grip tightened.

The man in the leather jacket stripped to his shorts, and made a leap-dive into the water. One of his companions followed, running in close behind him. The two men swam vigorously, cheered on by the men on shore. The dogs bayed out of control.

When the swimmers reached Brown and the coffin, the man in the lead hollered, "Brown! You ol' fool! What yo' gonna do with that coffin? You cain't take it from a church like that! The Reverend, he say . . ."

Brown's screams echoed through the forest. "I don't care what the Reverend say! The chile is mine!" He grappled with the two who tried to wrest the coffin from him. "I'll kill you!" he cried. "With my bare hands!" A huge fist rose up and pummeled down upon one man, who dived quickly under water. He surfaced a few feet away, unhurt.

"You gone crazy, Brown?" The other man asked. "Haven't you had enough of killing?"

"I'm gonna bury Bellinda," Brown replied.

"We know you couldn't help what you did," the man said. "But that child should be buried proper!"

"You killed my chile!" Brown's eyes grew enormous.

"We didn't kill your child," the man said.

"I seen it with my own eyes!" Brown yelled. "I remember. Oh, Lawd. Why'd you let them do it?" Brown gave the coffin a push. One of the men grabbed him around the neck. He gasped for air, then went under.

"Where'd he go?" the other man said.

"There!" his friend shouted, pointing to a huge back rising ten feet ahead of them. "He's getting away!" They swam after him, but Brown was rallying all his strength. He had to reach the opposite shore. The little coffin was bobbing wildly up and down in front of him. Then suddenly Brown screamed and stopped swimming.

He looked back at his tormentors, who held off pursuit. "Brown?" the lead man said. "You all right?" There was no reply. They waited, not knowing whether or not to continue towards him. His voice was heavy as he struggled for breath.

"I didn't mean no harm," he gasped. "I just wanted to take Bellinda home." He looked upwards as if trying to see something that could not be seen. One hand clutched tight to his chest, the other hand slid slowly off the coffin top. "Brown done gone, honey," he whimpered. He sank slowly.

The two men swam fast towards him. One dived under the coffin, and after a few seconds came back to the surface. "Cain't find him," he said, "must've sunk clean to the bottom." The other man dived, too. He surfaced, and dived again. They couldn't find Brown. They began pushing the coffin back toward shore. The dogs were still baying as the men on shore helped drag the coffin from the water.

"Better pry off the lid to make sure ever'thing's okay in there," one said. When the coffin lid was taken off, they fell silent, and the dogs, smelling death, shut up.

They stood gazing at the small, brown body. "Looks like she's asleep, don't it?" the tall man said. Then one of the swimmers knelt down and touched the brown face. "Lawd keep yo', Bellinda Belle Brown. Yo' daddy is with you now."

"All of 'em's dead now, ain't they, Brother Hawkins, "the other swimmer said.

"Yes," Hawkins replied. "These are bad times. Grief is a

killing thing." Then he stood up, and started dragging the coffin back toward the water.

"You gone crazy?" cried the man with the dogs. "You ain't gonna sink that little girl, is ya?"

"She's dead, Ben," he said, "and she was all Brother Brown had left. Brown didn't want a church burial nohow. He never was much of a believer. Poor Brown would sooner turn ta the devil than the good Lawd for help."

"Now hang on there, Brother Hawkins," Ben said moving nearer. "Brown hardly talked to anybody, you know that. How do you know what his beliefs was or wasn't? If he really was a disbeliever, then his little girl would need a Christian burial ta make sure she gets her foot through them pearly gates."

"Ben," Hawkins said. "By now, this little girl's already gone through them gates. So no matter where she's buried, nor how, ain't gonna make no difference." He slowly pushed the coffin to the water's edge. One man picked up the lid, and several others began gathering rocks.

They carefully placed the rocks in the coffin all around the little body. Then Brother Hawkins reset the lid, and rock-tapped it shut. He and his fellow swimmer took off jacket and trousers, and walked into the water. They buoyed the coffin in their arms, and slowly waded out.

Ripples creased, pressed, convulsed. A man on shore took off his hat. Someone bowed his head in prayer. Hawkins and his friend unclasped their hands, letting the coffin tip and sink. "Lawd have mercy, please," Hawkins said. Then, seeing it sink from sight, they swam back to shore.

Some women had gathered there with the men, and several held blankets. Hawkins and his friend were wrapped in them, when they climbed out of the water. Reverend Thomas was there, too, his Bible tight in his hands.

"I have just been told what happened here," Reverend Thomas said trembling. "And I am asking you to come with me now to church to ask the Lord to forgive you for what you have done. How could you bury a child without a minister? Brother Hawkins. You have committed a sin greater than you know."

Hawkins stood silent. He looked from face to face of the solemn standing group. He looked skyward. "Reverend," he said. "Brother Brown was so griefstricken, he didn't know what he was doing nor saying. He even accused us of killing his child. Well, maybe we did. We never got to know him. None of us, Reverend, not even you."

Reverend Thomas moved closer. "Every man is to come to God of his own free will," he said, his voice quivering. "Brother Brown did not, so that child was buried in sin. Good Lord, Brother Hawkins! Whatever possessed you, a God-fearing man?"

"Go back to your church, Reverend," Hawkins said. "Go back and pray that we find Brown's body in the morning. Pray for Bellinda's deliverance to heaven. Pray for Brother Brown. Pray that he finds rest from his torment, the torment of having accidentally killed his own child."

"He was a heathen and a conjurer!" Reverend Thomas said, spitting the words into Hawkins' face. Hawkins said nothing. He slipped into his trousers and jacket. Reverend

Thomas looked around anxiously for someone else to speak up. No one did. He turned on his heels, and walked off toward town.

After a short while, others began drifting back to town. It seemed that there was nothing more to see, nothing more to say, or do, at least not until morning. Hawkins and Ben with his dogs led their group back to the ridge. The heavy stamp of their steps shook the earth and rose into the hollow sound of the wind. Finally they began to speak. Brother Hawkins' voice rose above the rest.

"Brown didn't know that the brew he had stirred up for Bellinda was poison, not medicine."

Another voice chimed in, "Poor ol' man, trying to live all to himself."

And another, "He shoulda' known better. Where do you suppose he got his ideas?"

The voices fell hush. Then the voice of Ben Davis rose up. "I think, maybe, from the Bible. Doesn't it say somewhere in Jeremiah . . . ?"

His voice trailed off. The dogs bayed and barked, and tugged at their leashes. Then, in the soft hush of a wind, and the gentle laps of the water against the shore, silence yawned.

SONIA SANCHEZ

After Saturday Nite Comes Sunday

It had all started at the bank. She wuzn't sure, but she thot it had. At that crowded bank where she had gone to clear up the mistaken notion that she was $300.00 overdrawn in her checking account.

Sandy walked into that undersized-low-expectation-of-nig-gahs-being-able-to-save-anything-bank. Meanly. She wuz tired of crackers charging her fo they own mistakes. She had seen it wid her own eyes, five checks: four fo fifty dollars, the other one fo one hundred dollars made out to an Anthony Smith. It *wuz* Winston's signature. Her stomach jumped as she added and re-added up the figures. Finally she dropped the pen and looked up at the business-suited/cracker sitten across from her wid crossed legs and eyes. And as she called him faggot in her mind, watermelon tears gathered round her big eyes and she just sat.

Someone had come for her at the bank. A friend of Winston's helped her to his car. It wuz the wite/dude who followed Winston constantly wid his eyes. Begging eyes she had once called em, half in jest, half seriously. They wuz begging now, along wid his mouth, begging Sandy to talk. But she couldn't. The words had gone away, gotten lost, drowned by the warm/april/rain dropping in on her as she watched the car move down the long/unbending/street. It was her first spring in Indianapolis. She wondered if it wud be beautiful.

He was holding her. Cryen in her ear. Loud cries, almost louder than the noise already turning in her head. Yeh. He sed between the cries. He had fucked up the money. He had . . . he had . . . oh babee. C'mon Sandy and talk. Talk to me. Help me babee. Help me to tell you what I got to tell you for both our sakes. He stretched her out on the green/oversized/couch that sat out from the wall like some displaced trailer waiting to be parked.

I'm hooked he sed. I'm hooked again on stuff. It's not like befo though when I wuz seventeen and just beginning. This time it's different. I mean it has to do now wid me and all my friends who are still on junk. You see I got out of the joint and looked around and saw those brothers who are my friends all still on the stuff and I cried inside. I cried long tears for some beautiful dudes who didn't know how the man had em by they balls. Babee I felt so sorry for them and they wuz so turned around that one day over to Tony's crib I got high wid em. That's all babee. I know I shouldn't have done that. You and the kids and all. But they wuz dudes I wuz in the joint wid. My brothers who wuz still unaware.

I can git clean babee. I mean I don't have a long jones. I ain't been on it too long. I can kick now. Tomorrow. You just say it. Give me the word/sign that you understand, forgive me fo being one big asshole and I'll start kicking tomorrow. For you babee. For the kids. Please say you forgive me babee. I know I been laying some heavy shit on you. Spending money we ain't even got—I'll git a job too next week—staying out all the time. Hitting you fo telling me the truth bout myself. My actions. Babee it's you I love in spite of my crazy actions. It's you I love. Don't nobody else mean to me what you do. It's just that I been acting crazy but I know I can't keep on keepin' on this way and keep you and the children. Give me a whole lot of slack during this time and I can kick it babee. I love you. You so good to me. The best muthafucking thing that done ever happened to me. You the best thing that ever happened to me in all of my thirty-eight years and I'll take better care of you. Say something Sandy. Say you understand it all. Say you forgive me. At least that babee. He raised her head from the couch and kissed her. It was a short cooling kiss. Not warm. Not long. A binding kiss and she opened her eyes and looked at him and the bare room that somehow now complemented their lives and she started to cry again. And as he grabbed her and rocked her she spoke fo the first time since she had told that wite/collar/cracker in the bank that the bank wuz wrong.

The-the-the-the bab-bab-bab-bies. Ar-ar-ar-are th-th-th-they o-o-o-okay? Oh my god. I'm stuttering. Stuttering, she thot. Just like when I wuz little. Stop talking. Stop talking girl. Write what you have to say. Just like you used to when you wuz little and you got tired of people staring at you while you pushed words out of an unaccommodating mouth. Yeh. That wuz it she thot. Stop talking and write what you have to say. Nod yo/head to all of this madness. But rest yo/tongue and nod yo/head and use yo/hands till you git it all straight again.

She pointed to her bag and he handed it to her. She took out a pen and notebook and wrote that she wuz tired that her head hurt and was spinning and that she wanted to sleep fo a while. She turned and held his face full of little sores where he had picked fo ingrown hairs the nite befo. She kissed them and let her tongue move over his lips, wetting them. He smiled at her and sed he wud git her a coupla sleeping pills. He wud also pick up some dollies fo himself cuz Saturday was kicking time fo him. As he went out the door he turned and sed lady, you some lady. I'm a lucky mothafuka to have found you. She watched him from the window and the sun hit the gold of his dashiki and made it bleed yellow rain drops.

She must have dozed. She knew it wuz late. It wuz dark outside. The room wuz dark also and she wondered if he had come in and gone upstairs where the children were napping. What a long nap the boys were taking. They wud be up all nite tonite if they didn't wake up soon. Maybe she shud wake them up but she decided against it. Her body wuz still tired. She heard footsteps on the porch.

His voice wuz light and cracked a little as he explained his delay. He wuz high. She knew it. He sounded like he sounded on the phone when he called her late in the nite from some loud place and complimented her fo understanding his late hours. She hadn't understood them, she just hated to be a complaining bitch. He had no sleeping pills but he had gotten her something as good. A morphine tablet. She watched his face as he explained that she cud swallow it or pop it into the skin. He sed it worked better if you stuck it in yo/ arm. As he took the tablet out of the cellophane paper of his cigarettes, she closed her eyes and fo a moment she thot she heard someone crying outside the house. She opened her eyes.

His body hung loose as he knelt by the couch. He took from his pocket a manila envelope. It had little spots of blood on it and as he undid the rubber bands, she saw two needles, a black top wid two pieces of dirty, wite cotton balls in it. She knew this wuz what he used to git high wid.

I-I-I-I-I don-don-don-don't wa-wa-want none o-o-o-of that sh-sh-sh-shit ma-a-a-a-a-n. Ain't th-th-th-that do-do-do-dope too? I-I-I-I-I just just just just wa-wa-wa-nnnt-ted to sleep. I'm o-o-o-kay now. She picked up her notebook and pen and started to write again.

I slept while you wuz gone man. I drifted on off as I looked for you to walk up the steps. I don't want that stuff. Give me a cold beer though if there's any in the house. I'll drink that. But no shit man, she wrote. I'm yo/woman. You shudn't be giving me none of that shit. Throw the pill away. We don't need it. You don't need it any mo. You gon kick and we gon move on. Keep on being baddDDD togetha. I'll help you man cuz I know you want to kick. Flush it on down the toilet. You'll start kicking tomorrow and I'll git a babysitter and take us fo a long drive in the country and we'll move on the grass and make it move wid us cuz we'll be full of living/ alive/thots and we'll stop and make love in the middle of nowhere and the grass will stop its wintry/brown/chants and become green as our black bodies sing. Heave. Love each other. Throw that shit away man cuz we got more important/beautiful/things to do.

As he read the note his eyes looked at hers in a half/clear/ way and he got up and walked slowly to the john. She heard the toilet flushing and she heard the refrigerator door open and close. He brought two/cold beers and as she opened hers she sat up to watch him rock back and forth in the rocking chair. And his eyes became small and sad as he sed half-jokingly, hope I don't regret throwing that stuff in the toilet and he leaned back and smiled sadly as he drank his beer. She turned the beer can up to her lips and let the cold evening foam wet her mouth and drown the gathering stutters of her mind.

The sound of cries from the second floor made her move. As she climbed the stairs she waved to him. But his eyes were still closed. He wuz somewhere else, not in this house she thot. He wuz somewhere else floating among past dreams she had never seen or heard him talk about. As she climbed the stairs, the boys' screams grew louder. Wow. Them boys got some strong lungs she thot. And smiled.

It wuz eleven thirty and she had just put the boys in their cribs. She heard them sucking on their bottles, working hard at nourishing their bodies. She knew the youngest twin wud finish his bottle first and cry out fo more milk befo he slept. She laughed out loud. He sho cud eat.

He wuz in the bathroom. She knocked on the door but he sed for her not to come in. She stood outside the door, not moving, and knocked again. Go and turn on the TV he sed, I'll be out in a few minutes.

It wuz thirty minutes later when he came out. His walk wuz much faster than befo and his voice wuz high, higher than the fear moving over her body. She ran to him, threw her body against him and held on. She kissed him hard and moved her body over his until he stopped and paid attention to her movements. They fell on the floor. She felt his weight on her and she moved and kissed him and moved and kissed him as his hands started to move across her small frame that wuz full of red/yellow/motions that reached out for Winston's yesterdays to turn them into tomorrows. Her body wuz feeling good and she culdn't understand why he stopped. In the midst of her pulling off her dress he stopped and took out a cigarette and lit it while she undressed to her bra and panties. She felt naked all of a sudden and sat down and drew her legs up against her chest and closed her eyes. She reached fo a cigarette and lit it.

He stretched out next to her. She felt very ashamed as if she had made him do something wrong. She wuz glad that she culdn't talk cuz that way she didn't have to explain. He ran his hand up and down her legs and touched her soft wet places.

It's just babee that this stuff kills any desire for fucking. I mean I want you and all that but I can't quite git it up to

SONIA SANCHEZ

perform. He lit another cigarette and sat up. Babee you sho
know how to pick em. I mean wuz you born under an un-
lucky star or sumthin? First you had a niggah who preferred
a rich/wite/bitch to you and blkness. Now you have a junkie
who can't even satisfy you when you need satisfying. And his
laugh wuz harsh as he sed again, you sho know how to pick
em lady. She didn't know what else to do so she smiled a
nervous smile that made her feel, remember times when she
wuz little and she had stuttered thru a sentence and the
listener had acknowledged her accomplishment wid a smile
and all she cud do wuz smile back.

He turned and held her and sed stay up wid me tonite
babee. I got all these memories creeping in on me. Bad ones.
They's the things that make kicking hard you know. You be-
gin remembering all the mean things you've done to yo/
family/friends who dig you. I'm remembering now all the
heavee things I done laid on you in such a short time. You
hardly had a chance to catch yo/breath when I'd think of
sum new shit to lay on you. Help me Sandy. Listen to my
talk. Hold my hand when I git too sad. Laugh at my fears
that keep popping out on me like some childhood disease.
Be my vaccine babee. I need you. Don't ever leave me babee
cuz I'll never have a love like you again. I'll never have another woman again if you leave me. He picked up her hands
and rubbed them in his palms as he talked and she listened
until he finally slept and morning crept in through the shades
and covered them.

He threw away his works when he woke up. He came over
to where she was feeding the boys and kissed her and walked

166

out to the backyard and threw the manila envelope into the middle can. He came back inside, smiled, and took a dollie wid a glass of water. He fell on the couch.

Sandy put the boys in their strollers in the backyard where she cud watch them as she cleaned the kitchen. She saw Snow, their big/wite/dog come round the corner of the house to sit in front of them. They babbled words to him but he sat still guarding them from the backyard/evils of the world.

She moved fast in the house, had a second cup of coffee, called their babysitter and finished straightening up the house. She put on a short dress which showed her legs and she felt good about her black/hairy/legs. She laughed as she remembered that the young brothers on her block used to call her a big/legged/momma as she walked in her young ways.

They never made the country. Their car refused to start and Winston wuz too sick to push it to the filling station fo a jump. So they walked to the park. He pushed her in the swing and she pumped herself higher and higher and higher till he told her to stop. She let the swing come slowly to a stop and she jumped out and hit him on the behind and ran. She heard him gaining on her and she tried to dodge him but they fell laughing and holding each other. She looked at him and sed I wish you could make love to me man. Then she laughed and pushed him away and sed but just you wait till you all right Winston. I'll give you a work out you'll never forget and they got up and walked till he felt badly and they went home.

He stayed upstairs while she cooked. When she went upstairs to check on him, he was curled up, wrapped tight as a child in his mother's womb, and she wiped his head and body full of sweat and kissed him and told him how beautiful he wuz and how proud she wuz of him. She massaged his back and went away. He called fo her as she wuz feeding the children and asked for the wine. He needed somethin' else to relieve this saturday/nite/pain that wuz creeping upon him. He looked bad she thot and she raced down the stairs and brought him the sherry. He thanked her as she went out the door and she curtsied, smiled and sed any ol time boss. She noticed she hadn't stuttered and felt good.

By the time she got back upstairs he wuz moaning and turning back and forth on the bed. He had drunk half the wine in the bottle, now he wuz getting up to bring it all up. When he came back up to the room he sed he was cold so she got another blanket for him. He wuz still cold so she took off her clothes and got under the covers wid him and rubbed her body against him. She wuz scared. She started to sing a Billie/Holiday/song. Yeh. God bless the child that's got his own. She cried in between the lyrics as she felt his big frame trembling and heaving. Oh god she thot, am I doing the right thing? He soon quieted down and got up to go to the toilet. She closed her eyes as she waited fo him. She closed her eyes and felt the warmth of the covers creeping over her. She remembered calling his name as she drifted off to sleep. She remembered how quiet everything finally wuz.

One of the babies woke her up. She went into the room and picked up his bottle and got him more milk. It wuz while she was handing him the milk that she heard the silence. She ran to their bed/room and turned on the light. The bed wuz empty. She ran down the stairs and turned on the lights. He wuz gone. She saw her purse on the couch. Her wallet wuz empty. Nothing wuz left. She opened the door and went out on the porch and she remembered the lights were on and that she wuz naked. But she stood fo a moment looking out at the flat/Indianapolis/street and she stood and let the late/nite air touch her body and she turned and went inside.

EVAN K. WALKER

Harlem Transfer *

He shot the Browning Automatic Rifle down into the crowded street, and the people did not move. The bullet slammed into the hood of a new lavender Eldorado Cadillac dappled with snow, and not a soul moved. He shifted his position in the window and aimed the BAR at a hustler outlined against the dirty gray snow near the curb. The rifle was aimed at the center of the man's head, but before he fired he raised it a click. The bullet tore a large hole in an overstuffed garbage can out of which scurried two large rats—one white, one black—which ran into the deserted house across the street. Then the people on the crowded street in the middle of Harlem moved, moved as if they had been jolted from a deep sleep, and found cover in the cellars, hallways and stores.

As he saw the hustler crawl into the Lucky Dollar Bar and

* *Harlem Transfer* first appeared *Black World*, May 1970.

Grill, he smiled and moved back from the window. The smell of cordite stung the air in the small living room, and it made him think of the last time he had fired the BAR, many years ago in a land he barely remembered. It flashed across his mind in pieces and fragments, fragments and pieces—of snow, of valleys and of mountains, always mountains, seemingly strung out across the face of the earth. He looked at the BAR and rubbed his hand over the steel and wood, freshly oiled and cleaned, and it felt good.

Down on the street he could see that a few people had come out of their hiding places. He thought this strange but passed it off as curiosity; anyway, they had nothing to fear from his rifle; Dap was not among them. But Dap would soon come out of the Lucky Dollar Bar and Grill. Of this he was sure. Several men had gathered around the lavender El D and were talking and pointing to the hole in the hood. From his sixth floor window he could not hear what they were saying, nor did he care. He smiled. They probably think one of them rats ate that hole in that Caddy, he thought. And he waited by the window, calmly, quietly, quietly as he had been trained to do light years ago, to wait in the snow in a land that was now only disjointed pieces and fragments reforming themselves into meaning in his mind.

He saw the Dapper Dude come out of the Lucky Dollar Bar and Grill, walk coolly over to his El D and rub his hand over the wound in its hood. Dap took off his hat and scanned the buildings, his sleepy eyes bare slits against the blazing yellow sun. Then Dap kicked the dirty gray slush with his slick alligator shoes and bared his teeth toward some ungodly thing that he could not see and under his breath he said, "Some motherfucker done shot my El D."

Up on the sixth floor, the man with the gun aimed carefully, breathing in and then breathing out as he squeezed the trigger, as he had been trained, and saw the top of Dap's head fly through the air and land on the wound in the hood of his lavender El D. The red and white blob did a little shake dance and then was still. He switched the BAR to automatic and ripped off a burst that plowed into Dap's heart and turned his yellow coat into a bright orange. The sun caught Dap for a second, and then fell into the gray streets.

He left the smoking barrel of the BAR sticking out of the window until he was sure someone—it was, in fact, a junkie who had been strung out since Bird died—had seen where the shots came from. That ought to get a little action 'round here, he thought. That ought to bring Bull runnin'. But maybe the bastard off threatenin' some whore over on 125th Street for some money. Yeah, that be just like Captain Bull. I be givin' him a chance to be a hero and he be off blackjackin' some hustlin' woman in the name of the law and the Christmas spirit. Well, one thing for damn sure; he got his last Christmas gift from Dap. Fact is, Dap ain't gon' lay nothin' on nobody no more. Come on Bull, you bastard. Come on and see what a airconditioned skull look like.

A shroud of silence lay stiflingly across the street below. Never during the eleven years that he and his family lived there had he seen such stillness. Silence. Not a hustler wrote a number; not a junkie nodded; not even James Brown wailed from the record shop. Silence. And he never felt so good as when he looked down on the Dapper Dude, not so dap now, and saw a white rat scurry away from what was left of his head. Even the rats, he thought, don't want his ass now.

He lit a cigarette and sat in his overstuffed chair and watched the silent, flickering images on the television set. A children's chorus was singing Christmas carols, songs praising the young Lord who had come to deliver the people from eternal bondage. Even with the sound turned down, he knew the song they were singing. He had learned it from his mother as a child in Georgia, and he had taught it to Bobby, his only son. He remembered that the song never failed to bring tears to his eyes. He rose from the chair and turned up the sound, and the children's voices rang into the dark, close little room and seemed to shake the picture of the Christ child that hung behind the set. They sang about peace, love and eternal deliverance from suffering. But this time no tears came to his eyes. He sat down in his chair and waited.

There was nothing to do but wait. The first part of his plan was completed. After seventeen years, the BAR worked perfectly; his eyesight, as he had feared, had not failed; his aim was as good as the day he qualified as a master marksman in advanced infantry school. The clips of bullets lay neatly spread out on the coffee table. The gas mask was on the floor near the window. He had made his choice, the time had come, and now he walked the lonely passage that men must taken when their grief turns to anger, and that to solitary action; when they can no longer depend on man or God for redress of their grievances. And he neither wanted nor expected the help of either. But most important of all, he was not afraid.

He had felt the absence of fear many times, especially when he was thousands of miles from home firing his BAR and taking the unending snowcapped mountains for reasons which he only vaguely understood. Once, it was after they had taken Mountain 999, he asked his young captain why they had taken the mountain, what was its strategic importance. The young veteran of more than two hundred campaigns around the globe—his wite face was streaked with blue and red blotches, the result of, so the rumor went, locked bowels—took off his helmet and narrowed his pale eyes, hitched up his pants and said, "We are taking these mountains, boy, to rid the world of our enemies!"

Warming to his subject, he went on: "In the course of human events, we and God have decreed that it is our moral right to make the world a fit place to live in. And, boy, when you got moral right in your heart and a gun in your hand, anything is possible. Anything . . ." The young captain would have undoubtedly told him more, the very secret of the universe, but the order came from the general to take Mountain 1000, and the young captain led the troops down the mountain exhorting them to their moral duty: "Charge! Charge! Ye defenders of decency, charge!"

The young captain, a merciless commander, drove him up the next mountain, drove him to stalk the padded figures and silently slit their throats. "A slit for decency. Good show, my boy," he said. One of the figures, shot through the eye, pleaded for mercy, begged to be spared. The young captain leaned into his ear and said, "Do your moral duty, boy. Your country demands it." And he laid down a heavy burst into the enemy's good eye with his BAR. As they marched across the endless mountains, the young captain gave him a bright green gas mask; and he was indifferent to the stench of death even among the severed arms and heads and legs freezing in the falling snow, soon to be forgotten, not even remembered by God, who, wearing his dark shades and squinting from behind the sun, watched as the young captain whispered to him that he was the true king of the world and God was on his side. With this, God split for lunch.

Now, sitting in his thick overstuffed chair smoking a cigarette, he did not even feel the last traces of outrage; they had vanished after he and his wife, Mae, had gone, to no avail, to the police precinct for the tenth time, and then finally, still hopeful, downtown to the hundredth floor offices of N.E.G.R.O., the Negro Enigmatic Grievance Research Organization. He and Mae stood before the chief of N.E.G.R.O., Pimpleton, who seemed to listen patiently, benignly, as they explained their grievances, but was secretly looking past them and out of the window, perhaps wondering if the low clouds meant more snow and his flight to Miami Beach would be canceled. His attention vaguely drifted back to the couple before him.

". . . So you see that cop captain up there, he in on it too," Mae said.

"Won't lift a finger. Talk to us like we ain't in our right minds," he added.

Pimpleton smiled benignly and said, "What more proof I need? Everybody in Harlem know it."

"But my dear sir, N.E.G.R.O. cannot, nor I as chief of N.E.G.R.O., move on such flimsy evidence." Pimpleton sucked on his pipe as if it were a warm sugar tit and went on. "I mean, my dear sir and madam, things simply are not done that way. The gravity of your charges beg to be substantiated by facts. Facts, not hearsay, are the only means by which N.E.G.R.O.—and I am N.E.G.R.O., to state it bluntly —can move. By the way, do you belong to N.E.G.R.O.?"

"I can't afford to belong to N.E.G.R.O."

"A pity."

He clinched his fist and looked at the little old negro seated in his large leather chair behind his ten-foot mahogany desk. What kinda game this joker think he tryin' to run on me, he asked himself. He wanted to strangle Pimpleton's wrinkled little chicken-skin neck.

But instead, he said, "You got lawyers supposed to work for us; let 'em check it out. I'll show 'em where to look for facts, evidence, as you call it."

"My dear sir, you can't expect N.E.G.R.O. to go off on a wild-goose chase, as it were; we can't unleash our lawyers on speculation. We must have reasonable faith that we will be successful. Heavens to Betsy, what would our board of directors say? That is the foundation of N.E.G.R.O., success in the mainstream!"

"Bullshit."

"I beg your pardon."

"I said, bullshit!"

"Oh, oh, yes. But we must remember that everything has its time and place. We must not become impatient. Justice is certainly not blind; she is sometimes tardy but never blind."

He smiled as he looked at the shrunken little man, his Brooks Brothers suit about three sizes too large for him. He bared his big white uneven teeth and bloodred gums and thundered into Pimpleton's face: "Pimpleton, fuck justice. I think the bitch needs bifocals. Fuck her! Funny time-dressin' slut. Fuck her!"

Pimpleton sprang up from his chair like a shot, his sunken little eyes jumped to attention and twitched in step, and he wiped the spit from his narrow little head with his spotless white handkerchief. He was shocked. Shocked! Shocked that there were still half-crazed niggers raving about their mythical grievances, niggers who were beyond redemption, beyond ever swimming in the mainstream to which he had devoted eighty years of his life. "Well, sir, Washington was not built in a day, neither was Calcutta for that matter. But we must perservere, mustn't we? Godspeed and good day, sir."

And with that, Pimpleton did a quick shuffle from behind his desk and ushered them past rows of pictures of himself shaking hands with presidents and out of his office. As they departed, he imagined that Pimpleton went back to his mahogany desk and with trembling hands poured himself his fifth shot of Chivas Regal that morning. He smacked his thin little lips and got back to plotting what he would say to the

178

Concerned Citizens of Miami Beach in his everlasting quest for funds to research and eradicate grievances. He wondered about his accommodations; he would accept nothing but the best. The couple who had stood before him only seconds before were now faint shadows floating on the dark side of his mind.

The next morning Mae sat stiffly at the kitchen table. She had not touched her breakfast, and it lay limp and cold on her plate. She sipped some water and was careful to avoid looking at the empty chair to the right and at her husband sitting opposite her. He lighted a cigarette, sipped his coffee, and watched the vein jump on the back of her hand.

"I don't seem to have no appetite in the morning," she said, trying desperately to smile through the pain that seemed permanently engraved on her face.

To look at her like this, to see her redrimmed eyes pleading for answers he could not give her, lashed his soul. But he managed to smile and say, "You got to eat something, baby. You ain't gettin' tired of your own cookin', good as it is, are you?"

She smiled weakly and picked at her food and noticed that he had eaten only half of his eggs. "There ain't," she said, calmly, evenly, "nothing we can do, is there?"

"Don't say that, Mae."

"It's like don't nobody care. Like we hangin' off on the edge of the world and everybody stompin' on our fingers."

"Don't say that, baby."

She forced herself to look at the empty chair and said, "They took our hope away and ain't nothin' we can do."

He held his right hand, hoping that she would not see it tremble.

"I wouldn't bring no more into this world; same thing happen to 'em—just like Bobby."

"Mae, Mae, baby . . . don't say that."

"It's all fixed. Nothin' we can do."

"The hell there ain't."

"What can I, you, anybody do?"

"I'm gonna . . ." He caught himself. It was better that she know nothing of his plans.

"What we need," she said, her voice detached, seeming to come from outside her body, "is a god or somebody who got us in mind when he plannin' and plottin' the way things suppose to go down."

"Come on, baby. If I'm gonna drop you by Sara's 'fore I go to work, we better be makin' it."

She did not move. She just sat there looking through him, beyond him, her eyes angrily riveted on the picture of the Christian savior hanging above the television set in the living room.

"It'll be better for you at your sister's today. She'll be good company for you."

He took his wife down into the street. The wind, blasting from the west and across the river, blew the heavy snow into their faces; and for a moment they were blinded by it. But they wiped the snow from their eyes, leaned into the west wind and walked up the street. On the corner, through the driving snow, they could see the lavender El D parked, its motor running, and through the windows they could see the two men seated inside; one a thin black blur dressed in yellow, a cigarette slanting from his thick lips; the other, a fat ghostly white dressed in dark blue. They walked on. They said nothing. She because she thought all hope was gone. For him words were no longer of any use.

In front of Mae's sister's house he kissed her, holding her closely and tightly to him. Mae felt the tightness of his grip and wondered why it had such urgency. She looked into his face, but it told her nothing. He gave her an envelope and told her not to open it until Christmas. She smiled, and he kissed her lovely face again. He watched her walk into the apartment house and to her sister. He turned and walked quickly home.

He butted the cigarette and noticed that the sun had crossed the river and was dropping quickly behind the hills. He rose from the chair and slowly became aware of the noise coming from the street below. He was not surprised. It takes a little longer, he thought, when it ain't nothin' but a dead nigger laid out in the street. He crossed to the window and saw that the street was filled with people, many crowded around Dap's body, now that the police and ambulance had come. Four cops, wearing white riot helmets, bullet-proof vests and carrying rifles and tear gas guns, had jammed a junkie up against the wall near the Lucky Dollar Bar and Grill. The junkie was talking slowly and pointing to a building near the end of the block. Bull was not among the cops.

"Sonofabitch," he muttered to himself. "Come on, let's get it on." Then he glanced down to the center of the block, in front of the record store, and saw a mobile television unit. Its crew was busy shooting the scene. One cameraman was moving in to shoot Dap's body as it was being loaded on a stretcher by two attendants from Harlem Hospital. Do it in color, man, do it in color. Maybe some of these other bastards get to thinkin' 'bout how they messin' with they own folks. He spat out the window.

And then he heard it.

He heard it before he saw it. And he felt in his bones, knew beyond all doubt, that the siren signaled that his man was coming to him. His head suddenly felt light and giddy. And only when he picked up the BAR and watched the police car roar into the block and stop in front of the ambulance did his excitement leave him.

Captain Bull stepped out of the car. The brass buttons on his blue uniform pierced the gray twilight like cats' eyes. He, too, was dressed in flack jacket and helmet and carried a Thompson sub-machine gun at high port.

From his window he zeroed in on the gold captain's bars on the front of Bull's helmet, and was about to squeeze off a round when a black newscaster, that station's roving black reporter in Harlem, stepped in front of Bull and began to interview him. He lowered his rifle and cursed under his breath. Time. I got plenty of time, he thought.

Bull, flanked by his sergeant, the newshawk and his cameraman, walked to the ambulance. Bull stopped the attendants just as they were sliding Dap's body into the ambulance. Bull pulled back the sheet and looked at what was left of the man called Dapper Dude.

He had been watching the scene below so intently that, at first, he had not heard the voices. Voices that were familiar to him.

"Do you know this man, captain?"

"I've never seen him before in my life."

"Do you have any idea who killed him?"

"No."

"Why would anyone want to kill him, any idea?"

Then he turned around and saw that the scene below was being televised live and in color on the evening news. Ain't that a bitch, he thought. Good. Let the whole fuckin' world see it.

"The work of a madman, I'd say."

"Shit!" he said. "But you right; I'm mad as a bitch." He turned back to the window and saw Bull nod to the attendants, and they shoved Dap inside and slammed the door.

He saw that Bull and his sergeant were now joined by four cops. They pointed to the junkie. The junkie nodded and still pointed to the building near the corner. Bull led his men in that direction. In the gray twilight, he caught Bull's white helmet in his sights. He led him, one, two, three; fired. He missed. He missed Bull's head by less than an inch. Bull dived under Dap's El D. His men scurried into the dark hallways and cellars. "Sonofabitch," he said. He switched the BAR to automatic and laid down a heavy field of fire at the El D. Nothing moved. Then he saw Bull rise on the street side of the El D and he squeezed the trigger. Click.

Click. Click. He moved to the table. He threw a clip into the BAR and another into his pants belt. When he returned to the window, he saw Bull and his men scurry into the apartment house directly across the street.

Well, that's that, he thought. It gonna go down different than I figured. Bull got to get him some high ground if he figure on takin' me. But he don't know I know that. Fool. He think I'm just some crazy nigger. Shit. I got right in my heart, a gun in my hand, and I'm the king of the world. Let's get the shit on.

He was sure the police knew exactly which window he had fired from. There would be no doubt in their minds; the last shots would frame it there forever. But he would not be in that window. He walked to the kitchen and was looking to the roof tops across the street when he heard Mae's voice. "Yes, that's my apartment."

He turned around and saw Mae and the newshawk on the television set in the living room. She was being interviewed behind the mobile unit downstairs. "Baby, watcha doin' down there? Goddamn!"

"You're sure the shooting came from your apartment?" the newshawk asked.

"I told you once, yeah."

"You also said the gunman is your husband?"

"Yeah, he my man. My husband and my man."

"Can you tell our audience why your husband . . . he has killed one man and is now engaged in a shootout with the police. Why?"

"He doin' what he's got to do."

184

"Er, er, I don't quite understand."

"He has to do what he's doin'. Nobody would understand."

"What kind of man is your husband? Had he been distraught, upset about something?"

Mae drew her thin black coat around her shoulders and clutched the manila envelope to her breast. The snow fell into her hair and crowned it with a strange majesty in the gray twilight, and she seemed to grow taller than her five feet two inches, and he knew she would be all right. Nothing could touch her now. Her eyes were no longer red. She looked carefully, clearly and directly into the newshawk's eyes and said, "He just a man. Just a man who had a son and lost him and didn't nobody care. He just a man, my man."

Mae looked lovely to him, a queen, and he loved her more than anything in this or any other world. He wished he had told her so more often. And tears came into his eyes; not tears of sadness or regret, but of a terrible completeness of the order of things, their rightness in the universe. He saw the envelope in her hand and knew its contents: his G.I. insurance of $10,000 which he had kept after his discharge; his paid up life insurance from the Georgia Life Assurance and Burial Association which his mother had taken out shortly after he was born; the money he had withdrawn— $252.43—two days earlier from the small bank account he had opened for Bobby to give the boy the little stake in life which he, the father, had never had; and the broken halves of his Combat Infantry Badge. Why he put the medal in the envelope he was not quite sure. It had been in the cigar box in the bottom of his trunk with his papers, the blue background peeling off, leaving the rifle a stark white against the silver. And, without thinking, he picked it up and broke it easily in his large hand and dropped it into the envelope.

"Does your husband belong to any organization?" asked the newshawk.

"He don't belong to nobody but himself . . ."

The first volley of shots, coming through the living room window, hit the television set, splitting open the image of Mae's head, and the television was silent. The next volley hit the picture of the young Christ hanging above the television set and riveted it to the wall. "Ain't that a bitch," he said. "They done nailed J.C. to the wall with an overdose of America."

He crawled to the kitchen window and cautiously looked across to the roof tops. There were two of them, their funny little white helmets pinpricks against the gray sky. He stood to the side of the window and fixed them in his mind's eye. The rifleman was on his left, the tear gas man on his right. He estimated the range and elevation, kept in mind that Bull and the other cops would try to break out from their hiding place, and whipped into the window, caught the rifleman about to squeeze off again, and blasted him. He knew the cop was dead and did not bother to watch him fall from the roof; instead, he laid down a sheet of fire in front of the door and into the hallway to keep Bull at bay until he was ready for him. He turned and caught the last cop in his sights just as the cop was about to fire his tear gas gun. As he saw the cop's head explode, he smelled the acrid, pungent odor of tear gas in the living room.

186

He plunged into the living room, his eyes quickly tearing, and put on his gas mask. While he was doing this, he did not, could not, see Bull and the four remaining men dart quickly across the street and into his building, their gas masks already on. But he heard them. He heard their outraged, stamping feet as they raced up the stairs. And he knew they could not wait to get him. So he decided to make it easy for them; he unlocked the door to the apartment; then, threw a fresh clip into his rifle and calmly knelt behind the overstuffed chair and aimed at the door.

He was somewhat pleasantly surprised at Bull's methods. Even though the door was cracked, he found it necessary to shoot the lock with his sub-Thompson. You anxious fool. Well, blast on, man, he thought, blast on in.

They rushed the apartment, firing at everything in sight, which was mostly smoke, and he caught them as they entered and he fired into the four limp bodies without thought of mercy. Then he looked at them sprawled on the floor, their faces hidden behind green gas masks. Bull's helmet had been blown off, and he moved through the gray smoke among the still arms and legs and blown away faces, and saw that Bull had worn a wig. He pulled the mask from Bull's face and thought that he looked curiously like a fat old woman.

Then he heard the sirens and threw another clip into his Browning Automatic Rifle, and he waited as he had done many years ago in a land of unending mountains. Fuck 'em all. Fuck every goddamn one of 'em, he thought, as he moved back to the window.

EDGAR WHITE

Sursum Corda (Lift Up Your Hearts) *

One evening in the city. The day of which had held more than the usual dreariness.

I had risen in the morning as per usual, summoned from sleep by the atonal call of my mother. Crawling out of bed, I found the sun existing between the soiled curtains of the window. It was quite unoriginal, quite repetitious. It was the eight a.m., sun, and little good could be expetced of it and me.

I probably found my uncle occupying the bathroom. Oh, I forgot. You don't know my uncle. My uncle was one Philip Simmons, who, after several unsuccessful assaults on the white man's world of commerce and profit, now inhabitated a small orange room adjacent to my own. (He imagined himself at whiles to be bestriding a large pogo stick in hell.)

* *Sursum Corda* first appeared in *Liberator*, December 1968.

Seated for breakfast (mother always gives a large breakfast, believing it to be the most important meal of the day),
was my sister. One arm at her chin, her face upturned toward nothing at all. She had beautiful brown eyes and an
oval face, all of which is quite unimportant to all save my
own recollection. The stained tablecloth gave off an odor of
burnt plastic. My mother tried, bending over my shoulder,
to deposit cereal and eggs in our respective plates. Thickly
strong hands, vein-filled, which I seem to remember as upturned and supplicatory.

After the meal came the walking of Dog (a useless, constantly barking animal). Down the long dark staircase, out
of the tenement house (by way of overstepping the prone
bodies of junkies), then out into the street.

Doggie busies himself about the befoulment of other dog-
gies. I lean against the building, watching smog gather in
the sky over gray unimportant houses.

Doggie satisfied, we together ascend stairs back into apartment.

My mother again bent over table, involving herself in the
perpetual folding of small paper bags.

My mother producing sepulchral drawn face, which con-
notes the beginning of a homily. And a homily did, in fact,
come. "What do you intend to do with your life?" she began.
I scratched my scrotum, anticipating the next line. "Why
don't you get a job?"

"I'm busy attending school," I responded, presenting my
altar boy face.

"I know you're going to school. Don't you think I know

you're going to school? After school, I mean, like other boys."

The prospect of work, any form of labor, filled me with perfect nausea. (I think it necessary here to say that what I had wanted to do, that is, always wanted to do, was to die. To die being that quaint state of inaction, cessation of body function, videlicet perfect perishment.) The thought of labor in a supermarket, moving among and beneath portly and dishonest foremen or fellow workers was utterly ludicrous.

I made my exit by means of pleading lateness to school. I was always late to school. School being high school. School being also absurd.

My father (no doubt you wondered about my father) was named Nephtali, as am I. The last image I have of my father is of a rather tired-looking negroid gentleman, with a mustache, wearing a soiled T-shirt bearing the cognomen COCA-COLA COMPANY.

One day I, being age six, arrived home from some delinquency or another to find my aforementioned father in the act of bringing his thin arm full circuit to place a fist in the immediate vicinity of my mother's jaw. Whereupon she slammed into the wall. He then, quite composedly, walking like an usher in a concert hall, entered the kitchen and in an orderly fashion proceeded to smash all the dishes. Finished, he spun on his heels, opened the door, turned and uttered succinctly: "And I'm never coming back." And, in fact, he didn't.

I arrived in school (a dull, tedious place with bad lighting and a multitude of unworking clocks), seated myself and began to attempt the simulacrum of a student. I was, however, immediately told by a short fat semi-moronic teacher (whose name I have never learned) that I had to report to the Dean of Boys for absence. The fact being that I had missed more than half the school year, a moiety of which I had forgotten how I spent. The Dean of Boys (since he must be described) was a robust Italian gentleman named Cappilo. He had the face and body of a retired boxer. Mr. Cappilo was also a pig and the Dean of Boys, and I was in trouble again.

"Nephtali, you've been absent for over forty days this term, and we've only had sixty-seven days so far. Where the hell have you been?"

"Well, sir . . ."

"Well, what was wrong with you?"

"Gout."

"Gout?" He disbelieved me. A truant officer had been sent to my home, etc., etc.—all of which is very dull. I must say in all truthfulness that I have learned absolutely nothing in school. Which puts me ahead, since most lose what they originally come in with.

The afternoon after school: walking through the series of ghettoes. The Ukrainian ghetto, the Puerto Rican ghetto, the Italian ghetto. All absurd, all loud, asymmetrical, burlesque. Like my confrontation with a white gang. Ritualistic exchange of abuse reaching a climax with the attempted kick to the ass. The grimace, the tightening fist, the gestures betokening anger. Out into the middle of the street, myself pretending equipoise. Only five of them, fortunately fighting one at a time. The Misericordia Church to the right. The serene face of the Madonna looking on in perfect detachment.

Overhead a middle-aged white woman calls out from her window: "Why here in front of the house? Drag him away from here; I don't want my little girl to have to see this stuff."

One of the members of the gang responded with an unfortunate obscenity. Myself moving about like a rag doll giving the occasional hit to the stomach, jab to the mouth series. Regretting greatly that I could not get into the apartment of the aforementioned woman so I could push her out of the window and perform a series of indelicate acts on the body of her little girl.

Police eventually come (being summoned), tell us to break it up in halfhearted fashion. Wanting very much to see me crucified by these boys. (Apparently I am not beloved by the New York City Police Department, a thing I find most odd.)

Police leave; fight resumes. I, much to my sorrow, throw one fellow headfirst to the ground. The others, seemingly disquieted, now all attack at once. A skillful parry; a daedal hand movement followed by a swift retreat between two closely parked cars. I attain a clear streetway. Id est: I fled. The folly of pursuit, involving the ludicrous huff-puff of the lungs and mouth; the praxitelean felxion of the elbow. The otiose rise and fall of the legs.

Once home I found my uncle again speaking to himself in his small orange room. He seemed in agreement this time. My sister was occupying the bathroom. My sister always occupied the bathroom, save for those times when Uncle Phil made existence there.

Thinking now of sister (a very small-bodied girl with even teeth and almost constant smile), it seems that she was the only one in the comedy who was not wholly farcical.

She managed her comings and goings. Went steady with a long boy who did laudable things on the school basketball team. Of late she has married an X-ray technician who owns a large car. Now their underwear abuts on an extended clothesline in the Bronx. My sister's name is Carol; soon they will have a daughter named Cathy. Quite uncomplicated.

In my mother's room, on the left wall, over the bed, and contiguous to several crucified palms, hung a marriage photograph (in sepia tone) of Mom and Dad. What could my mother have been thinking at that time? I cannot hear her voice as a younger woman. The lower lip seems hectic. Doubtless she was in a rush to get on with her new life. An escorted life with apparent security. The entire photograph softened, organized and rarified by a skillful photographer who actualized their collective dreams.

Outside my room, on the fire escape, lived Mrs. Thompson's cat. Mrs. Thompson lived upstairs and wrote large letters to her son who was imprisoned in a large jail. The letters were received and sometimes answered, after a fashion. Young Thompson (named Bill) once upon a time had had a girl friend named Jane who also had an occasional boy friend named Bobo. One evening Bill's green trousers and pointy black shoes came in contact with Bobo's sharkskin suit and brown shoes and they were disturbed at each other's existence. Jane (who was accompanying Bill) tried to pretend she was not in ecstasy at the sight of two men fighting over her. Bobo stabbed Bill. Bill bled. Bobo left to the muted applause of the Harlem onlookers. Several days later Bill sought Bobo out. Bobo was found. Bobo was shot, fell dying with contorted and moronic expression on his face. All of which is very operatic and quite unreal, save for the fact that Bill was then placed in the aforementioned jail to which his mother sent the large letters.

But these letters are important—in so far as anything is important—at least to the two people. (Forgive me, three, since one must remember the censor whose sole function it is to oversee the wording of various missives lest an obscenity and/or plans of escape be mentioned.) The sending of letters, the desideratum of which I believe to be communication. Several times Mrs. Thompson showed me some of the letters. In the upper lefthand corner was the word "relationship," apparently answered by the word "mother."

Mrs. Thompson also had two other sons. One named Ralph and one named Charles. Ralph perished in Vietnam. Charles, aged nineteen, was thus spared dying because of a peculiar but fortunate clause which allows only one son a war to a family. Mrs. Thompson's life was not wholly happy.

I sat in my room. On the floor. Far as I could into the corner. Sitting thus, my elbows could touch both walls and I could be in contact with everything. I tried to imagine the size of my penis at birth.

Outside, the complacent bells of the Catholic Church rang out. Puerto Rican girls making novena. The scent of their oiled hair. Their voices low and conspirational. The dim, flickering candles, serenescent and moving with their voices.

The Monsignor Russell had of late passed on to the better place. The parishioners felt cheated: he had quit them, like the candles. I remember Mother telling me of his death one evening while we were eating dinner. She pushed the bones of her fish to the outermost circle of her plate and moved her lips saying, "But you know he really was very nice, though . . . though you had a very hard time following him in the text, he mumbled so." Then she placed her chin on her hand. My sister always follows.

I liked the two corners of my room. With my elbows resting so against the walls, they (the walls) would feel quite soft. I sat there and listened to the sounds of my uncle breathing in the next room. There was a trick that I had mastered of changing bodies with him. I could do it also with the Spanish girl who I used to do moist things with, up on the roof. I would think for a very long time about the construction of their bodies and their gestures. I would copy my uncle's humped back and the intervals of his breathing. With Anna, I thought of what the weight of her breast must feel like, or the round buttocks, and of giving off a smell like she does. Soon we would change bodies, just like transubstantiation or something. I always wanted to be Anna's teeth.

But it was the evening I was really speaking of, wasn't it? Yes, it was that evening that a certain idea entered that portion of my worthless anatomy, which they call my head. The idea, or more properly the desire, came upon me to mount a greased pig. A pig of great enormity. And I and my pig would move through all the streets of the dead city. And this would be no ordinary pig, for its walk would be dainty as a woman's. Touching ever so lightly into gutters, its front hooves of terra cotta. Watching the tired ladies coming out of Harlem Hospital, nurses with thick heels, attendants swinging strange gray packages. Hearing their voices in the city night, a city of dulcitude and ash. But my pig could deal with them, the sepulchral or the merry. The girls sitting out on fire escapes, their silhouettes in the lighted windows, looking like caryatids. My pig understands so much; it would not question anything. It would be quite content with being fed, occasional copulation, occasional large trough, eventual regeneration. My pig understands so much. I would have a stable of pigs, eugenically bred. Give them to the multitude as I passed. One for Mother with the words COCA-COLA COMPANY on the mantle, one for Mrs. Thompson, one for her deceased son with the words IN ABSENTIA on its mantle, one for Uncle Phil bearing the word SUCCESS on its mantle, one for the Puerto Ricans, one for the Jews, one for the Italians, one with a curled tail for the *BLACKS*. I knew then—I did not want to know but I knew—that ragged dance which I did, along with the finite number of people who environed me, was, in fact, my life. One can exchange circuses by changing distances. One can not escape circuses.

I went to sleep that night in my clothes. I shut my eyes. Ran through a series of faces, some demented (a one-legged *gryllos* that stood in the corner bothered me most). A benevolent pig, a group of penitent sinners flagellating themselves, an Amish farmer, a soldier, a policeman, a building afire from which a child was leaping. Colors now. All green. Straight sound. Silence.

WALLACE WHITE

Kiss the Girls for Me

Lying in bed after a long hard day of chasing the bag, I always had the feeling that some great disaster was about to happen. Here was I, twenty-one and *knowing* that the world was suddenly coming to an end. The reality of it would come when she touched me. Her voice would come from some distant planet;

"I love you."

"I love you too." (Get your fucking hands off me, bitch.)

"George . . . why don't you like to have sex with me?"

"I don't know Lita, it just seems I'm always tired." (Bitch, you're a nymphomaniac!)

"George, you know we can't go on much longer like this."

"I know, I know—just give me a little more time." (This bitch thinks the bed is a battlefield—*Blood, sweat and tears.*)

We lay quiet for a while, me in my world of fear, as I knew she was trying to get me to fuck her. Suddenly I became aware of her hand stroking my swipe, her breathing coming in short, hungry sounds. Desperately I searched my mind for some past erotic scene to arouse my sleeping dick. Somehow I knew with that sixth sense that always forecasts doom, that tonight would see the end of our eight-month relationship.

Frantically, I tried to suspend reality, but her voice was insistent, passionate.

"Please, George . . . please . . ."

I pretended to be asleep. I could feel her grasping my joint, which was as limp as freshly cooked spaghetti. And I tried to light my memory, to summon up the energy, the potency that I knew was not there. Memories are strong, and I felt again my first shot of dope, I remembered how my mother had pleaded with me, cried, tore out her hair and finally kicked me out of the house for stealing everything that wasn't nailed down. And now I was facing a defeat as complete as any I would ever know. In the arms of my woman, heroin had proclaimed its victory.

(Maybe I can pick an argument and get her off my back.) I moved her hand from between my legs and sat on the side of the bed; I could see pure hatred in her eyes as I lit a cigarette.

"Look Lita—are you some kind of sex maniac? Every night I'm not in bed five minutes before you're trying to take my shorts off."

She jumped out of bed as if she had been held down by a coiled spring.

"Why you sonofabitch—me . . . a sex maniac? You act like

a homo. We've had sex exactly three times in the eight months we've been here! Meanwhile, I'm the one who pays the rent, buys the food, gets your damn clothes out of the cleaners, plus gives you money to buy that shit you use. Now, just because I want some sex once in a while, I'm a sex maniac—you about a jive bastard!"

"Shut up, bitch!"

"Shut me up, motherfucker!"

I jumped up. I turned to her and said: "Look bitch, I'm a man—I don't have to stay here and take your shit."

"You're damn right. Do me a favor and disappear."

I walked over to the clothes closet, snatched a suitcase off the shelf and put it on the bed. When I turned back to the closet, she was blocking the door. In her hand she held a butcher knife. I looked at her, and her eyes told me she was ready for combat.

"You black bastard, you ain't taking anything out of here but your black ass!"

All the excitement had brought my high down. Soon I would need another fix, and I didn't have any dope in the house. Anyway I wasn't in any condition to fight. I grabbed my coat off the chair, putting it on as I walked towards the door. As I opened the door, a heavy ash tray just missed my head and through the closed door I could hear her screaming, "Just forget my address, you fucking creep!"

As I hurried down the stairs, I heard her put the chain on the door. Once outside, the hawk put its cold arms around me. My first impulse was to go back upstairs and apologize, but then it dawned on me—I still couldn't make the sex scene. I walked. I felt the snow seeping in my shoes; my toes had become numb with cold. I spotted an open bar, and rushed in. One of my six dollars bought me a drink, and as I sipped slowly, I tried to figure out my next move. The bartender broke into my thoughts.

"The guy at the end of the bar wants to know if you'll have a drink with him." Grateful at being befriended when I was friendless, I answered by reflex.

"Sure."

By the time the bartender had finished pouring my drink, the guy had taken the stool next to mine. For the first time, I noticed that we were the only customers in the bar. We made small talk, and I put him down as a lonely guy looking for someone to talk to. After our third drink, he said, "Why don't we go up to my place?"

"Okay," I said.

We got in his car and drove uptown, not speaking during the short ride. Once inside the apartment, he fixed drinks. As he drank his drink, he kept looking at me; then he said, "Look—since the night is so bad, why don't you spend the night with me, if you don't mind sleeping with me."

He laughed a short embarrassed laugh as he said this. I could dig where he was coming from and it got me uptight. I had to squash it, not because of my great morals, but because, for the second time tonight, I would be called upon to perform the sex act and I knew I would flunk out again. I set my drink down on a small table and said, "Look man, I dig where you're coming from, but I got the claps."

At first he looked disappointed, then relieved.

"Oh—I'm sorry to hear that." He said this with such sadness you would have thought I had told him I only had six months to live.

"Anyway George, I wouldn't worry too much. With today's modern inventions in medicine, having the claps is like having a bad cold. After a couple of shots you'll be as good as new." The whole time he was talking, he kept looking at his watch.

"Perhaps I can drop you off at the subway." As he said this, he moved towards the door.

Outside, I felt a sense of victory and defeat—victory at protecting some image of my manhood, and defeat at not being able to make any money out of all of this. As he let me out at the subway, he handed me a bill and said, "Now you take care of yourself." He drove off and he didn't look back.

I looked at the bill and my heart leaped. It was a ten—I would be able to survive another day. I'd buy three bags of dope and sleep in some basement. Things would work themselves out by tomorrow.

Biographies

JOHN BARBER: 34 and married to Virginia (Stallings) Barber, New Haven, Conn. schoolteacher. Educated in Pontiac and Detroit, Mich. public schools. B.A. Morehouse College, and M.A. Yale University. *Some involvements:* New Haven, Conn. NAACP President, 1961-1964. Clashing with New Haven Police and Mafia gambling interests tooth and nail. Executive Assistant to SCLC President Dr. M. L. King, Jr. (1965-1966). Currently Special Assistant to SCLC Operation Breadbasket's National Director, Jesse Jackson. Long string of arrests for trespassing and disturbing the peace in civil rights demonstrations. Subject of prize-winning Yale Bio-Documentary *I Am a Man* 'bout me rioting and clashing with Conn. cops and courts and stuff.

VAL FERDINAND: born march 24, 1947 in New O., La. am married & have a daughter (ASANTE SALAAM). she is a gemini, my wife is a leo. i work with young brothers between the ages of 5 and 16 at a community center. we teach them reading, writing, arithmetic, black history, recreation, etc. plus brotherhood, discipline, unity

& the 7 principles. am managing editor of *The Black Collegian* magazine which is about black college students. am co-editor of NKOMBO Publications and am director of BLKARTSOUTH, a black theater movement that is an outgrowth of involvement with the Free Southern Theatre. i would like to hear from brothers and sisters everywhere so that we can grow more, grow closer, grow wiser. write me at NKOMBO Publications, P.O. Box 51826, New Orleans, La. 70150. Asante. PEACE&LIBERATION.

LIZ GANT:
liz
she's a little thing/has to reach up
ontoes
for sugar and salt and kisses
but standing/brown feet flat on the ground
projects thoughts that soar
so giants need wings to get where she is
                    (mervyn taylor)

R. ERNEST HOLMES: Born Harlem, July 24, 1943, in the midst of a racial battle in Harlem set in the context of World War II. It seems as if I have never lived without war of one sort or another. My credentials as an employee mean nothing in my capacity as a writer. Therefore, I will not state them. Suffice it to say that I am an eclectic and a universalist; that I have experienced too many memorable moments with peoples of all cultures to believe that hate is inherited; that I have seen too many black people surge back from seeming defeat for me to ever cease from struggling; and that it is *terribly* important in this life to have someone (parents, spouse, lover, friend or pet) who loves you.

ARNOLD KEMP: Born Miami, Fla., bred Harlem, New York. H.S. dropout at 15. Hustled. 4 years of USAF. Discharged. Hustled. Busted (Armed Robbery). Convicted. Sentenced (10-12 years).

Finished H.S. in prison. Paroled after 7½ years. Entered Queens College, N.Y. in 1967. B.A. in English in 1970. Now attending Harvard Graduate School, Cambridge, Mass. One produced play: *White Wound, Black Scar*. A few poems appear in anthology *We Speak As Liberators: Young Black Poets*. First novel due out any second.

AUDREY M. LEE: Born and raised in Philadelphia. Am growing old waiting for that train. Published work:
> Poetry in *Saturday Evening Post* and *Hartford Courant*
> Short Stories in *Negro Digest (Black World)*, *Essence* Magazine
> Novels: *The Clarion People*, 1968. *The Workers*, 1969.
> McGraw Hill. Have just finished another novel.

JOHN MC CLUSKEY: Born in Middletown, Ohio in 1944. Married and have a son. Presently I am teaching courses in Black Literature at Case-Western Reserve University in Cleveland, Ohio. I graduated from Harvard University in 1966 and have attended Stanford University. "The Pilgrims" is an excerpt from a chapter of a novel in progress.

THOMAS MULLER-THYM: Was born on December 23, 1948 into a large family (have four brothers and four sisters) and grew up in Harlem on 118th Street. Received a good education at Catholic schools, including four years of Latin and three years of French. Began smoking marijuana at eleven. Through ten years of drug use, including five years of heroin addiction, I was involved in almost every drug known to man, especially the drugs of the hallucinogenic variety, to which I became exposed at college. Though I had a habit in college, I managed to complete almost three years with an A average, but I was forced to drop out because after a while I couldn't keep up with the work. I have not yet returned to school to get my degree, and doubt that I ever will, because college is a fantasy—nothing compared to the reality I have been living since I left and entered the real world.

I have been drug free now for one year and three months, and plan to pursue a full time career in writing—I am being paid to do certain types of writing for the agency I work for now. It is a start in the right direction. I am working on a series of short stories right now which deal with my childhood on 118th Street, and will seek a publisher when the whole series is completed.

WALTER MYERS: Like all Black artists, he is trying to survive artistically (and physically?) in an environment which seems as hostile to his art as it is to his Blackness. He has published in such Black periodicals as *Liberator, Black World, BlkArts South.* Has also produced a children's book, *Where Does the Day Go?* published by Parents' Magazine Press. Presently he is a member of the John O. Killens Workshop at Columbia.

LINDSAY PATTERSON: Is editor of *Anthology of the American Negro in the Theater,* and has contributed numerous articles to *The New York Times, Saturday Review, Freedomways, Writer's Yearbook* (1970), *Negro History Bulletin, Columbia University Forum,* and other publications. His fiction has been published in *The Best Short Stories by Negro Writers, Essence* Magazine, and other publications. In 1967, he was selected as one of twenty-nine "outstanding and promising" young writers to receive a cash award from the National Foundation on the Arts and the Humanities. He has lectured at Kent State University, Hunter College and Columbia. A native of Bastrop, Louisiana, he is currently working on his autobiography, *Diary of an Aging Young Writer.*

ERIC PRIESTLEY: Born December 16, 1943, one of four children. He graduated from Jefferson High School, then attended East Los Angeles College, majoring in English. He received his degree in Psychology in March 1970 from California State College, Los Angeles College. Was active in the Watts Writer's Workshop and Studio Watts. His poem *Can You 'Dig Where I'm Coming From* appeared in *Watts Poets* edited by Quincy Troupe. Presently he's working on a novel *God Is the Sun*, about the Watts writers.

ALICE I. RICHARDSON: Born and raised in St. Louis, Missouri, has lived in Washington, D.C., and is now living in New York City. She began writing poetry at an early age, and has won school awards for poetry. She has had film and drama reviews published, and has written, staged, and directed a one-act play for the New York University Heights Summer Theatre. She was recently among the finalists in the Columbia University Press experimental poetry contest. She is presently working on her Ph.D. in drama at New York University.

SONIA SANCHEZ: blk/woman/mother/teacher/poet author of *Homecoming, we a baddDDDD people* and *It's a New Day* (poems for blk/children) Has also written 3 one/act/plays: *The Bronx is Next, Sister Son/ji* and *Uh huh; but how do it free us.*

EVAN WALKER: I was born in Milledgeville, Ga. and now live in New York City. My plays have been performed in Los Angeles, New Orleans, New Haven, and Philadelphia. With Larry Neal I have written and original screenplay which is scheduled to go into production in the Spring of 1971. I am currently working on a novel and several short stories.

Harlem Transfer won the Conrad Kent Rivers Memorial Award presented annually by *Black World* as the best fiction of the year.

EDGAR WHITE: Born in the West Indies and raised in Harlem and the Bronx, N.Y. His plays *The Mummer's Play* and *The Won-*

derful Year have been performed at the New York Shakespeare Theatre, and *J. Walter Smintheus* at the ANTA matinee series.

His short stories have appeared in *Liberator, Black Review* and several anthologies. He is the author of *Underground* a volume of four plays published by William Morrow & Co., and he is presently working on a novel *The Etude* which will be published later this year.

WALLACE WHITE: I began using drugs in 1945, and continued using them until 1965. Almost exclusively I used heroin. As an addict, I followed several careers. I was a burglar until a fall from a five story rooftop trying to avoid the police. I then pursued a career as a forger until I was arrested, then finally I became a beggar on the subways until I came into Addicts Rehabilitation Center in 1965. I have been drug free since that time. I began experimenting with writing in prison, and have been working at it since, though it is primarily a pastime. My full time career is in rehabilitation. In 1968, three of my stories were accepted by *Esquire* magazine for publication entitled, "Three Crises in the Lives of Dope Fiends." I am also under contract for a novel with the Cybertype Publishing Company, which will deal with my life while using drugs.